Also by Jeremy Akerman

and available from Moose House Publications

Memoir
Outsider

Politics
What Have You Done for Me Lately? - revised edition

Fiction
Black Around the Eyes – revised edition
The Affair at Lime Hill
The Premier's Daughter
In Search of Dr. Dee
Holy Grail, Sacred Gold (due in 2023)

EXPLOSION

a novel

JEREMY AKERMAN

Explosion
© 2023 Jeremy Akerman

Cover art by the author
Cover design: Rebekah Wetmore
Editor: Andrew Wetmore

ISBN: 978-1-998149-16-2
First edition September 2023

2475 Perotte Road
Annapolis County, NS
B0S 1A0

moosehousepress.com
info@moosehousepress.com

We live and work in Mi'kma'ki, the ancestral and unceded territory of the Mi'kmaw People. This territory is covered by the "Treaties of Peace and Friendship" which Mi'kmaw and Wolastoqiyik (Maliseet) People first signed with the British Crown in 1725. The treaties did not deal with surrender of lands and resources but in fact recognized Mi'kmaq and Wolastoqiyik (Maliseet) title and established the rules for what was to be an ongoing relationship between nations. We are all Treaty people.

This book is dedicated to
my long suffering wife, Caroll Anne,
who tolerates my moods and tempers while writing.

This book is fiction. As they often say in the film business. "some scenes and events have been altered for dramatic purposes."

Most of the characters who appear in it were real, historical people. However, I have put words into their mouths and actions into their lives. Except where it was recorded, we cannot know what they did and said at the time. We can only guess. I have guessed in one way; no doubt others would guess differently.

Explosion

Jeremy Akerman

1

It was November, 1917. The year to date had been exciting due to some military successes and other welcome developments in what some were calling The Great War; but sad, wrenching and depressing because of lost battles with obscenely heavy casualties.

Worst of all, what created a constant, gnawing fear day after day was that there seemed to be no light at the end of the tunnel. Indeed, many could not even see that there was a tunnel at all through which mankind could travel in order to put an end to more than three years of the most brutal warfare and devastation.

April had brought good news when the United States Congress officially declared war on the German Empire, an act which offered potentially-unlimited human resources and materièl for the allied cause. This was generally celebrated, although some thought the Americans had left it too late, and wondered why they not also declared war on Germany's partner, the Austro-Hungarian Empire.

Also in April there had been ominous stories about German perfidy in facilitating the return to Russia of the Bolshevik revolutionary Vladimir Lenin. It was reported that the Germans had transported the Bolshevik leaders in a sealed train from Switzerland to Saint Petersburg in order to stir up mutinous discontent in the Russian army.

A month later, it was announced that the United States would land an expeditionary force in Europe, to be headed by the handsome, mustachioed General "Black Jack" Pershing.

Many were encouraged by an allied victory in October at Passchendaele, even though jubilation was tempered by the knowledge that almost three quarters of a million lives, including 4,000 Canadians, had been lost in securing a salient ridge only a few miles long.

For Jews, British Foreign Secretary Balfour's declaration in November in support of a Jewish nation in Palestine brought hope for a brighter day, but only if the war would bring an end to the Ottoman usurpation of the land which Jews had inhabited for over 3,000 years.

Some cheer was occasioned by reports that General Allenby was reported to be knocking on the very gates of Jerusalem, and that the Turks would surely be dislodged from that ancient, holy city, thus ending a 450-year rule by the Ottoman Empire

The fruits of German treachery were soon known to the world when, in November, the Bolsheviks seized power in Russia with the slogan "Bread and Land" and offered to surrender to the German High Command. On November 8, Lenin signed the Decree on Peace, which was approved by the Second Congress of the Soviet of Workers and Peasants, proposing an immediate withdrawal of Russia from the war.

Lev Bronstein, also known as Leon Trotsky, was appointed Commissar of Foreign Affairs in the new Bolshevik government and, with his friend Adolph Joffe, was designated to represent the Bolsheviks at the peace conference at Brest-Litovsk to be held at the end of December.

Also ominous was news of a stalemate at Cambrai, in northern France. The battle which had been raging since November 20 appeared as if it might be turning in the Germans' favour, the allies' use on a large scale of the recent invention, the tank, having met significant failure due to mechanical problems. The Germans were also pursuing Italian allies in a massive offensive at Asiago, the western end of their line, and gave all appearances of being ultimately victorious.

The Supreme Allied War Council was to meet in

Versailles, France at the end of the month to define their war aims, on which they had so far been unable to agree. If they could not concur on their reasons for fighting the Central Powers, the man on the street might well have been forgiven for thinking that it did not bode well for eventual success.

Were all this not sufficient to bring trepidation and despondency to the citizens of Halifax, Nova Scotia, the weather had been turning nasty for some days and the temperature was dropping. There was a cutting wind coming off the sea, which was difficult to escape and so made life miserable for any who had to be outdoors for any length of time.

What the people of Halifax did not need in their lives was more bad news.

2

Earlier in the war, the Allies had instituted a blockade across the North Sea in an attempt to limit the amount of war supplies, food, and fuel which could get to Germany from beyond its shores. Kaiser Wilhelm responded by instructing his Secretary of State, Admiral Alfred von Tirpitz, to devise and execute a plan to use submarines to destroy all ships supplying the Allies. These were *unterseeboots*, or U-boats, armed with torpedoes and deck guns.

It was one of these, U-20, which dramatically torpedoed the ocean liner *Lusitania* in 1915, when more than 1,200 men, women, and children drowned, and which helped to start a gradual change of opinion towards the war in the United States.

At the start of the war in 1914, Germany possessed fewer than 40 U-boats, but three years later there were 140 which had, between them, sunk over a quarter of the world's merchant shipping.

At the beginning of 1917 the German aim was to sink more than 600,000 tons of shipping a month, hoping to break the allied blockade of German supply ports.

Consequently, the U-boats were ordered to conduct unrestricted attacks against all ships in the Atlantic, including civilian passenger carriers, the German leaders thinking they could defeat the allies before the U.S. could mobilize and send troops to Europe.

In 1916, as part of this campaign, the U-53 under Korvettenkapitan Hans Rose had raided Allied shipping off the coast of Canada and the United States, although confining its activities to international waters.

Later, the German High Command decided to take the submarine war to North America, in a more serious fashion and commissioned larger Type U-151 and Type U-139 submarines. The first of these was armed with 18 torpedoes and two 150 mm deck guns, and had a range of 46,300 km, while the U-139 had 24 torpedoes.

Germany's development of this U-cruiser submarine allowed it to strike the Atlantic coast of its newly-declared enemy, the United States. The records say that the first German U-boat arrived in American waters in May 1918 and sank 13 ships, as many as six in a day.

By mid-1918 Germany had built 334 U-boats and

had 226 under construction.

German naval records show that the earliest sortie to North America by one of these larger submarines was in April of 1918, when Korvettenkapitän Heinrich von Nostitz und Jänckendorff took his U-boat to Chesapeake Bay where she laid mines off the Delaware capes, and cut the submerged telegraph cables which connected New York with Nova Scotia.

However, recently discovered documents (in private hands) have revealed that von Nostitz und Janckendorff made a test run across the North Atlantic in late 1917, and on November 29 of that year found himself several hundred miles off the coast of Nova Scotia.

Even in these larger German submarines, it was very dimly lit, dirty and claustrophobic, the fifty submariners on board not being able to change clothes or shower, and having to share two toilets which water pressure rendered usable only when the vessel was less than eighty feet below the surface. After as much as two months at sea, the stench of humanity was added to the miasma of diesel fumes and bilge water. Sometimes navigation charts rotted in the fetid air, and the men's feet became infected with mildew and nail fungus.

Initially, U-boats obeyed so-called 'prize rules',

which meant that they surfaced before attacking merchant ships, which allowed the crew and passengers to escape. This chivalry was rewarded by rendering the U-boats vulnerable to attack, a danger which was intensified after the British introduced warships disguised as merchantmen, armed with hidden guns. These so-called "Q-boats" were intended to lure U-boats within firing distance in order to sink them.

The use of Q-boats contributed to Germany's eventual abandonment of 'prize rules', and by the time the U-151 reached Canada's international waters, submarine warfare was very much a no-holds-barred affair.

It was the dead of night, and below a brooding sky a vast expanse of black sea relentlessly swelled and surged, its surface swirling with fog. The small, dark mass of a merchant ship was barely distinguishable on the horizon, but in the near distance the surface of the water was broken by a stream of bubbles and foam as the tip of the U-151's periscope emerged.

Below decks, a sailor, reeking with sweat and dirt after weeks at sea, peered into the periscope as he slowly and awkwardly revolved in the confined space. Kapitan von Nostitz und Janckendorff, the vessel's first officer, and a junior officer watched as the sailor made an almost-complete circle.

"Yes!" said the sailor, "There it is. I am almost sure of it."

"What is she? What can you see?" demanded the captain.

"There's too much swell. She's disappeared."

"Let me have it!" the first officer ordered. He strode over to the periscope, and squeezed in behind the instrument.

Through the sights, he could just make out a dirty old freighter coming in and going out of view with sea's roll. In a few minutes, the image was clearer and the vessel's hull became visible.

"It says 'Belgian Relief', captain."

"Can you identify her?"

"Just a minute. Wait. Yes, I can just make it out. She is the *Imo.* She is flying a Norwegian flag."

"Ah," said the captain.

"Let's take her," said the Second Officer. "Shall I prepare to fire the torpedoes, Captain?"

"No, let her go," Captain von Nostitz und Janckendorff replied.

"Are you sure, sir? She is a sitting duck."

"Quite sure," the Captain said.

"It wouldn't be any trouble, sir. We still have 15 torpedoes unused."

"I said no, Schroeder. Let her go."

Jeremy Akerman

3

In New York's Long Island, between Coney Island and Fort Hamilton, lies Gravesend Bay, a natural harbour sheltered from the open sea by the Seagate promontory. A stone's throw from the fort are the Verrazano Narrows, which separate Brooklyn's Dyker Heights from Staten Island, a quiet, rural place of woods and farms.

For years, New Yorkers had been regaled with plans to bridge the narrows, and even to link the land masses with a tunnel, but it had all come to nothing, and those who wanted to go for a drive in the country or to purchase fresh eggs had to take a ferry. When the ferry was out of action, the few who had urgent business on Staten Island had to go up the east bank of the Hudson River to the Livingston Bridge in Albany, then down through New Jersey to Elizabeth, there to take another ferry to the island—a journey of several days.

The first white people to settle in Gravesend were Quakers, who arrived in 1643 under the leadership of Lady Deborah Moody. They were granted land by Willem Kieft, the Governor of New Amsterdam, and there they settled and thrived.

For centuries the area was peaceful and relatively unpopulated, a condition which prevailed until the dawn of the twentieth century. When, in 1917, the United States declared war on Germany, the bustling shipping activity which existed in the Brooklyn docks and shipyards to the north spilled out into Gravesend Bay as increasing numbers of merchant and naval vessels were urgently required to prosecute the war. Also, since the declaration also meant the United States was now allied with Britain, France, Italy, Russia, Romania, Canada and Japan, it followed that Gravesend became a focal point for ships from allied countries to be repaired, equipped, supplied and victualled.

Thus, by the fall of 1917 Gravesend was a scene of endless activity, both of incoming vessels and ships sailing on foreign missions of a military nature. Recently there had been dramatic embarkations of thousands of American doughboys to relieve the occupation of Saaremaa in Estonia, and to face the enemy in German South West Africa.

Gravesend and Brooklyn were also ports through which thousands of tons of explosives were shipped, rendering the area less than safe in the minds of many local people. In 1916 an explosion at Black Tom Island of a vessel loaded with TriNitroToluene damaged the Statue of Liberty and was said to have been heard in Pennsylvania. The barges which brought the explosives to Gravesend Bay were required to anchor at least a thousand feet from shore and only three ships at a time were allowed to be supplied with dangerous materials.

The German U-boat campaign had sunk a significant number of French merchant ships, so the government of President Georges Clemenceau rounded up all available ships and pressed them into service. One of these was the *Mont Blanc*, which was registered in Saint Nazaire, and owned by the Compagnie Générale Transatlantique. She was 18 years old, 97 metres long and had a net capacity of 2,000 tons.

Towards the end of November, a slender, black-bearded man in his early forties, his kit bag slung over his shoulder, sauntered along the docks at Gravesend, searching for the office of the agent representing the French naval authorities in New York. The waterfront was alive with activity, and the air was filled with a cacophony of hammering, welding and riveting.

The man poked his head into this corner and that of the tumble of buildings until he found the makeshift headquarters of Monsieur Fernand Moreau, the agent.

He was a small, agile man with darting eyes and expressive hands who leapt up from his desk when he saw the man enter. "Captain Le Medec?" he asked.

"Bien sŭr, c'est moi," answered the man, slinging his kitbag onto the desk. "Aimé le Medec reporting for duty."

"You are welcome, Captain. Your ship is being provisioned as we speak. Here are your sailing orders." M. Moreau handed him a sealed package which the captain took and opened.

"England?"

"Yes, likely Southampton. You won't be told until you are at sea."

"What are her armaments, in case we do meet the enemy?"

"A light gun mounted forward and another aft. She is a single screw with a top speed of 10 knots."

"Will she be heavily loaded?"

"Oh, yes. Very heavily. You will not be able to go fast."

"About five or six knots at the most, I would guess."

"Yes. I would not think more than that. You'll be there in four, maybe five days."

"I'd better see her. Can we do that now?"

"Yes, of course, please follow me."

They went out on to the wharf and picked their way through a forest of ropes and cables until they came to an unimpressive grey vessel riding at anchor. Her depth markings showed that she was still more than half empty.

"Of course, in normal times the government would not employ a ship like this," said Moreau, "but we have lost more than 100,000 tons to U-boats in the last month alone."

"I've seen worse," said le Medec tersely. "Let's go aboard and see who I am going to be sailing with."

As they mounted the gangplank, heads appeared on deck and various officers and men emerged to greet their captain.

"Men, this is your new captain," announced Moreau. "Aimé le Medec. France expects you to serve him well."

"At ease, men."

"This is your first officer, Jean Glotin."

Le Medec nodded as the officer snapped off a salute.

"Second officer, Levesque."

Le Medec grabbed his hand and shook it warmly.

"You are acquainted?"

"Indeed we are. How have you been, Levesque?"

"Excellent, thank you, Captain. It will be a pleasure to serve under you again."

"Antoine Legat, Chief Engineer."

"Legat, I am pleased to make your acquaintance. How is everything below?"

"So-so, Captain, She is not a young mistress, so will not give us much vigour. One of the boilers needs to be watched, but I think she will get us to where we are going."

"Good."

"Incidentally, Captain, where *are* we going?"

"I'll tell you tonight after dinner. Do we have a cook?"

"Not yet," said the agent, "but one is one the way. Not, unfortunately, a French cook."

"Ugh. When will he get here?"

"Tomorrow."

"Well, men, we will have to fend for ourselves tonight. Permission is granted for all officers plus two hands to go ashore and see what food can be scavenged. We will assemble in the wardroom at six bells."

4

Halifax Harbour is ice-free in winter, varies in depth from 16 to 70 meters, and contains four islands, Devils' Lawlor's, McNab's and George's. Depending upon the point from which measurements are taken, this stretch of water is of varying widths and is about 15 kilometres long. It leads into Bedford Basin, an enclosed bay eight kilometres long and five kilometres wide. In order to get from one to the other it is necessary to sail through The Narrows, a passage less than half a kilometre wide.

It is thought that the harbour was formed millions of years ago by a glacially formed valley which later flooded after the ice age passed. Being strategically located, it is the first inbound and last outbound port of call in North America with transcontinental rail connections, and is two days closer to Europe and one day closer to Asia, via the Suez Canal, than any other North American East Coast port.

It was therefore a natural choice for the allied forces to use as the rallying and departure point for trans-Atlantic shipping convoys. The port had been under the control of the British government until 1905, when its dockyards and environs became the responsibility of the Canadian government; but with the war raging, a considerable presence of the Royal Navy could still be felt. That presence could be seen daily in the number of British ships in port and in the uniforms worn by the many sailors seen about town.

To protect anchored shipping in Bedford Basin, but not in the harbour itself, submarine nets were stretched across The Narrows each night and removed the next morning.

This day, both shores were lined with ships of all varieties: colliers, fishers, passenger carriers, port and pilotage vessels, merchantmen, and all manner of warships. Prominent among them were *HMS Highflyer, HMCS Niobe, SS Corfe Castle, SS Calone, SS Curaca, SS Middleham Castle, SS J.A. MacKee, SS* Hovland, and the sturdy tugs *Hilford, Lee, Gopher, Douglas H. Thomas*, and *Musquash*.

In Bedford Basin lay several dozen freighters and merchant vessels in formation, arranged in order that as many as possible could be accommodated without impeding the ingress or egress of any of them. These ships were of every conceivable shape and size, flying the colours of many nations, among them Canada, Britain, the United States, France, Norway, and Belgium.

High overhead towards the open sea was a small aircraft, its wings glinting in the sunlight. This was an experimental Curtis H2SL a so-called "flying boat", and it was proceeding north with the snowy Eastern Shore away to its port side, the vast expanse of sparkling Atlantic ocean on its starboard. The roar of the large, single engine, mounted above and behind the cockpit, was deafening to its occupants. One of the first of these planes to be produced, this was being tested by the United States Navy along with an experimental flight training camp on the proposed site of an air base at Baker's Point, just north of Dartmouth, the city across the Harbour from Halifax.

In the front seat was Emma Chambers, a beautiful young woman of 21. Only wisps of her blonde hair were visible poking out from her leather helmet. At the controls was Lieutenant Gabriel Hanson, a dark-haired, handsome man of 26. He and Emma had met only a few months earlier when she had arrived in Halifax, but they had formed a deep affection for one another and had been "keeping company" ever since.

Emma was the niece of Rear Admiral Bertram Chambers, the Port Convoy Officer and Senior Naval Officer Escorts. She had accompanied him to Halifax, along with her brother, Billy, and the admiral's wife, their aunt Nora.

Emma's parents had been 'unaccounted for' for over a year, having been last heard from in Tabriz in Persia, where her father was a diplomat. Apparently, they had become embroiled in a clash involving Persian, Turkish and Russian forces, and were believed to be dead. Under those circumstances, the admiral and his wife decided to adopt the siblings and to take Emma and William with them to Halifax when Chambers received his new posting in July of 1917.

Gabriel was in the act of banking the aircraft, so Emma could get a better view of a lone fishing vessel steaming towards the coast, when the engine spluttered. He tapped his gauges and pulled the choke. The engine sounded even worse and, after some deep guttural noises, cut out.

The plane now seemed to float on the clouds, gliding with its own momentum. The only sound was the icy wind whistling and howling around them. Gabriel reached forward and tapped Emma on the shoulder. With great difficulty she managed to partially turn to see him. He mouthed what looked like "too cold" and pointed to the surface to indicate he would take the craft down.

Hanging on to her seat in sheer terror, Emma watched as the plane dived sharply towards the temporary U.S. air base some miles away. She shut her eyes and prayed for deliverance as Gabriel skilfully followed the coastline for as long as he was able.

He struggled with the controls as eventually the water rose to meet them and the plane made a huge slapping sound as it made contact, only to be thrown back into the air by an enormous wave.

Emma screamed as, for a second, they could only see blue sky and clouds, then the aircraft slammed back into the sea with a loud splash. Shortly, all that could be heard was the lapping of the waves as they floated, rolling with the sea.

Gabriel ripped off his goggles, unbelted and hoisted himself up onto the fuselage. Emma had done her best to scramble out and sit on the edge of the cockpit.

"Are you alright?" he asked.

She took off her goggles and helmet, shaking out her magnificent, long golden hair. "I think so," she said, clearly shaken.

Gabriel reached out and touched her flight suit. "Maybe I should make an inspection to be sure."

She brushed his hand away with a laugh, and then became serious. "Do you love me, Gabriel Hanson? Really love me?"

"You know I do. We're going to get married, aren't we?"

"Then I want you to promise to stop flying. It's too

dangerous."

"Emma, you know I can't do that. You shouldn't ask what is not possible. It's war time and I'm in the service. The only way I could do that would be to disobey orders, then I would be shot for mutiny."

"Yes, I know," she sighed. "But I had to ask. What was wrong, anyway?"

"I think we were a bit too high and the cold is affecting the fuel lines. I'm just the pilot. The ground crew will figure it out. The plane is still in the experimental stages, which is when we are supposed to find out what the bugs are."

"Well, until those bugs are sorted, don't expect me to go up again!"

Just then they heard the sound of a boat coming towards them, and a shout. They had been spotted, and a crew from the base were now arriving to tow them back.

5

The Admiral's residence, overlooking the harbour, was a spacious, rambling, well-furnished Victorian house at the edge of the city's North End. A large vestibule, flanked by potted aspidistras, opened out on the right hand side, first to a rather sparsely populated library, then to a dining room with a highly polished table and eight elegant chairs. Directly ahead was a wide, sweeping staircase leading to the upper floor and attic. To the left, through a wide, door-less portal, the hall opened onto a very large lounge, or sitting room which was well lit by bay windows, adorned by curtains of white lace.

The admiral sat reading his newspaper in the chair closest to the hall, his nephew William studied at a small desk opposite his uncle, while the window was occupied by Nora, the admiral's wife, and her companion, Mrs. Hutchinson. On the floor, looking at pictures of cars, was the Chambers' son, seven-year-old Marcus. Sitting stiffly, in the corner of the room, was the admiral's ADC, Lieutenant Nigel Gilchrist, a vain, arrogant young man who fancied his chances as a suitor for Emma.

Rear Admiral Chambers carried the made-up title of 'Port Convoy Officer and Senior Naval Officer Escorts' as a result of a petulant spat between the British and Canadian authorities. The British wanted him to be the superior naval officer in Halifax, with the title of 'Senior Naval Officer Afloat', but because Chambers was not a Canadian, Canada's Minister of Militia and National Defence, Albert Kemp, was offended by the proposition. To assert his paranoiac sense of propriety, Kemp deliberately promoted William Story (who, ironically, was an Irishman) to Vice-Admiral and dispatched him to Halifax as Dockyard Superintendent to ensure that Chambers would not be the highest ranking officer at the port.

The admiral was 51 years old, tall, gaunt, rather stiff and with large ears. His entire life had been spent in the navy; he had commanded a number of vessels and was steadily promoted throughout his career.

Not that his record was unblemished, because in 1888 a collision between the brig *HMS Sealark* and the fishing boat *Gypsy* occurred when Chambers was Officer of the Watch on *Sealark*. The accident was deemed to have resulted from a want of seamanship on his part, but what disciplinary measures were taken are unknown.

A year later, Chambers was instrumental in the gunboat *HMS Watchful* running aground, an incident which was said to be a result of Chambers' "want of discretion." Neither of these unfortunate mishaps seemed to have deterred the Admiralty from continuing to elevate him in subsequent years. For the Admiral, already on the retired list at his own request, Halifax would be his penultimate posting.

In the curve of the bay window, Mrs. Chambers and Mrs. Hutchinson were sipping tea, sitting properly in upright chairs with a tiny table between them.

Mrs. Hutchinson was the widow of a Royal Canadian Navy captain who had been drowned at sea, and was a near neighbour to the Chambers. She had befriended the family as soon as they had arrived in Halifax the previous July, and had become a frequent visitor to their house.

Nora Chambers was not what she looked like. A lifetime with Bertram (or 'Mordie', as she playfully called him, his unusual middle name being Mordaunt) had given her a degree of ease and of occupying a position in society where people deferred to her. Her manners were perfect and she carried herself with dignity, but she had not always had such a life.

She had grown up on the wild, remote Falklands Islands, 300 miles off the coast of South America, which supported a coaling station for the British Navy. The islands, occupied by some 3,000 inhabitants, were often subjected to severe storms in winter, with an average rainfall which was often twice that of Halifax. Being so far from England, luxuries were few and far between, so Nora had no reason to develop 'airs and graces.'

Bertram was handsome enough in his uniform and she had been as attracted to him as he was to her. Their time together had been relatively happy, especially when their son was born seven years ago.

"I hear you are doing quite well at the Academy, William," the admiral said, looking up from his *Herald*. "What are you studying this week?"

"Rules and signals of passage, Uncle," said William.

"Ah, 'The Rules of the Road'. Well, you're not the first to find some of them a bit tricky and probably won't be the last. Are the instructors good?"

"Pretty good, for the most part. There's one, a retired boatswain, who is really good. We all like him."

"That's because practical experience invariably outweighs theoretical knowledge," said the Admiral. Then, calling to Glichrist, he asked, "Nigel, when is Murray due to report?"

"Eight bells, sir."

"Good. He can stay for dinner. You don't object, do you, Nora?"

"No, indeed. Why should I?"

"Let the kitchen know, will you, Nigel?"

Gilchrist left to go down to deliver the instructions, while Chambers went back to his paper.

"At least young William seems to have settled in very well," said Mrs. Hutchinson.

"Yes, he has," replied Nora. "I am very pleased with his progress. Marcus is doing nicely at school, too, although all he ever talks about is Cadillacs, Buicks, and Pierce Arrows."

"And Emma?"

"I am not exactly displeased with her. In a way, I think it quite admirable that she insists on working at the textile factory."

"She is in the office, of course?"

"Oh, yes. It certainly would not be proper for her to do manual work."

"I should think not!"

"There was never any question of that. She says she has to pay her own way, as she puts it. I think I understand, although it is not at all necessary."

"Did she inherit much when her poor parents died?"

"No, alas. The admiral's brother was in the diplomatic service, so his estate barely covered the funeral expenses. No, I meant that we can support her until she marries. She doesn't have to work if she doesn't want to."

"Maybe that American will take her off your hands," said Mrs. Hutchinson mischievously.

"Please don't say that! I have nothing against the young man. He is agreeable enough, and well-mannered for an American. It's just that he doesn't seem very steady, if you know what I mean. He strikes me as rather reckless."

"I suppose she is with him now?"

"Yes. Flying in an aeroplane, if you can believe such a thing!"

"Heavens!"

"I'm amazed the admiral allowed her to go up in that machine. He is usually so solicitous for her welfare."

"Hmm. An aeroplane! I see what you mean about him not being steady, my dear."

6

Out in the harbour, only a few miles from the admiral's house, was a large American freighter preparing to enter The Narrows in order to secure a safe berth in Bedford Basin. At the wheel was the port pilot, Francis Mackey, who had 23 years' experience on the water, being now in his mid-forties.

He was a sturdy, muscular man, balding, with a bushy moustache and a penetrating gaze. He had established a good reputation in the port, had a highly responsible job that was better-paid than most, and owned a modest row house in the city. His wife, Lillian, and their five children were well provided for. He had every reason to suppose that he was at the height of his natural powers, and that the future would be promising.

Mackey approached his job with complete confidence, being certain of his ability and his familiarity with the harbour and all its features. The ship slowly swung into the basin.

"Dead slow ahead!" Mackey commanded.

"Aye, aye, Mr. Mackey. Dead slow ahead," repeated the ship's master.

The third officer clanged the throttle, echoing the order. "Dead slow!"

"I'll take the berth between the *Morning Star* and the *Atlantica*," said Mackey.

"There's not a lot of room to maneuver," said the captain, sounding a note of caution.

"Don't worry, skipper, I've had lots of practice. I've got into tighter places than that."

The ship very slowly glided into the space between the other two vessels, stopped, and anchors were dropped. When she was made fast, Mackey relinquished the wheel to the captain and the two men shook hands.

"I shall see you again when you sail out," said Mackey. "It's a pleasure doing business with you."

"Goodbye, Mr. Mackey. See you in about a week."

Mackey swung out and climbed down the rope ladder to his pilot's boat, which seemed like a tiny cork bobbing against the hull of the freighter. The boat pulled away and headed back through The Narrows. Mackey turned from the wheel and gave a brief wave.

7

"It's a damnable state of affairs when the ship isn't provisioned until the cook arrives," observed Glotin bitterly.

"Maybe he wants to get into André Michelin's guide," said Le Medec sardonically, "and only the best of provisions will do for him."

"The agent said the cook is not French, so I wouldn't get your hopes up, Captain."

The two men sat on the wharf, smoking the new Gauloises cigarettes with their strong Syrian tobacco, and taking in the myriad activities all around them. Some of the ship's officers and ratings had gone off to find provisions for that night's dinner, but they had little hope they would be able to scavenge anything very palatable.

As they were sitting there, a team of longshoremen carrying a quantity of wooden planks boarded the *Mont Blanc*. The foreman barked some orders, directing the men to the forward holds.

"What the hell is this?" Le Medec asked. "You

know about this, Glotin?"

"No, Captain, but here is Levesque. Maybe he knows."

Levesque joined them, looking equally puzzled.

"Were you notified of this, Levesque?"

"Not me, Captain. It must be something the agent has ordered, though why they should need us to take wood across the Atlantic beats me."

Just then a grizzled old carpenter, a large sling of tools over his shoulder, passed by them on his way to the ship. In his free hand he carried a large, lidless, faintly clinking box. As he shifted the weight of his burden, a small item fell from the box.

"What is that?" Le Medec asked. "Glotin, go get it."

Glotin slid down from his perch and walked across the wharf. He bent down and picked up the fallen object. "Captain, it is a nail."

"A nail, that's all?"

"No, Captain. It is a copper nail."

Le Medec and Levesque instantly exchanged worried glances. More longshoremen carrying planks went by and boarded the ship.

"Captain," Levesque said hoarsely, "Look at their feet. They have rags wrapped around their boots!"

"Sacre bleu! Glotin, go and see what this is all about," Le Medec instructed. "I don't like the looks of this."

"Nor I, Captain," said the Second Officer.

In a few minutes a frowning Glotin returned. "They are lining the hold with wood, Aime."

"The hell they are!" Le Medec erupted. "Wait here. I am going to see the agent!"

Pulsating with rage, Le Medec stormed along the docks and burst into Moreau's office. "Let me see the manifest!"

"Ah," said Moreau warily, "I wondered when you would get around to that."

"Give it to me now!"

"Calm down, Monsieur. I shall get it from my safe. There is only one copy, and it stays here."

Moreau retreated to an enormous cast-iron safe at the rear of the room and, with his back to Le Medec, opened it, removed some papers, and then handed them to the captain.

Le Medec seized them and excitedly began to read their contents. "22,000 kegs of priric acid. What the hell is priric acid?"

"It is dye used on silks and wool. It gives them a yellow colour."

"What?"

"It is also used in the manufacture of explosives."

"*Mon Dieu*!"

"Read on, Captain," said Moreau quietly.

"250 tons of TriNitroToluene. Merde!"

"There's more."

"62 tons of gun cotton in wooden barrels. This is a floating armoury!"

"Oh, and I should say—it was too late to appear in the manifest—you are also to take 494 steel barrels of benzol."

"Is that the same as Benzine?"

"Yes, I believe so."

"*Putain*! I won't do it! It is out of the question. It is much too dangerous!"

"I think you will, monsieur," Moreau said with a steely glint.

"Oh yes?"

"May I remind you, Le Medec, that since 1914, the government of France has employed the law of 1849 to declare a state of siege for the whole of France, with maintenance of law and order and such police work passing to the military. Refusal to carry out an order would be treason under articles 213,218,223, and 238 of the Military Code and is punishable by death."

"*Cochon*! How dare you lecture me on my duty!"

"I am just the messenger, monsieur. I am the instigator of neither the laws nor the contents of your cargo. I too am under orders."

"Forgive me. I understand your position. I was taken by surprise. Shock, really."

"*De rien.*"

"Of course, this means that, with this load, we will not be able to achieve five knots. Even with convoy protection, we would be a sitting duck."

"That is beyond my remit," said Moreau. "I am sorry for your troubles. Captain Le Medec, if you would like to join Madame Moreau and me for dinner this evening, you would be most welcome."

"That is kind of you, but I have to eat with my men. That is, if they have managed to find anything to eat."

"Your cook and provisions will be here in the morning."

"Good. Thank you, Monsieur Moreau."

~

When Le Medec got back to the Mont Blanc, he immediately became tangibly aware of the delicate nature of his cargo, as he listened to dull thumps and cries of "Be careful with that, boys!" He could see that all of the workmen wore muffled boots and that none of them was using metal tools.

A man in civilian street clothes approached the ship and addressed him. "Captain Le Medec? Commander Martinson would like you to see him in his office."

"Who is Commander Martinson?"

"He is the senior British naval officer in New York in charge of convoys."

"I see. When would he like to see me?"

"Now."

"*Sanglant anglais. Toujours donner des ordres!*" Le Medec cursed under his breath. "Alright, lead the way."

~

Commander Martinson was an elegant, white-haired man in his sixties, in an immaculate uniform with a host of service bars glittering on his left breast. He sat behind a cluttered, but not untidy, desk, tapping out his pipe.

"Please sit down, old chap," he said in an upper-class accent.

Le Medec declined the offer and remained standing by the door. He did not intend to waste time on some effete bureaucrat.

"What is it?"

"You summoned me," Le Medec said. "I presume you have something to say about my ship."

"The *Mont Blanc*, isn't it?"

"Yes. You know that is my ship."

"Bound for Bordeaux via England?"

"Yes."

"Hmmm." Martinson made a show of carefully consulting some papers. "Maximum speed ten knots when empty. Likely five knots or less if overloaded."

"Yes. So?"

"I am afraid there's no nice way of putting it, old chap. You're much too slow for us. We can't take you in the next convoy. It has to maintain ten knots."

"*Quoi?*"

"Yes, I'm sorry. You can't leave with this convoy. I am going to have to reroute you."

"For God's sake! Where to?"

"To Halifax. That's in Nova Scotia. A much larger and slower convoy will be leaving from there in about a week's time. You can cross the Atlantic with that one."

"*Putain!*"

"Yes, it is rather hard lines, I'm afraid. I am most terribly sorry, but I couldn't possibly slow down an entire convoy for one vessel. I'm sure you under-stand."

Jeremy Akerman

8

In the admiral's sparsely-endowed library, Bertram Chambers and Lieutenant Commander James Murray R.N.V.R, the Sea Transport Officer, stood at a large table covered with charts.

Murray, in his early fifties, was a rather short, serious man with a large moustache, who had been at sea since 1879. He was a member of the Royal Naval Reserve and a Fellow of the Royal Geographic Society, and had the reputation of being a careful and punctilious officer. In his time, he had sailed the coast of West Africa, the Indian Ocean, the West Indies and South America. He had, in turn, been captain of *Lake Manitoba*, *Empress of Britain*, and *Empress of Ireland*. Murray had come to Halifax after being Harbour Master at Quebec

"I've never seen the port so crowded, Admiral. They're packed in like herrings in a box. And they're not all here yet."

"How many more do you expect?"

"Another eleven, sir, including the convoy escorts."

"Good God! Where shall we put them all?"

"There's still room in Bedford Basin for the freighters, if we are careful. And the new naval vessels will have to squeeze in among the wharves."

"I don't mind telling you, Murray, I don't like it one little bit. It is a recipe for trouble."

"We'll just have to be on our toes."

"Speaking of which, Murray, I have just had a message from Martinson in New York."

"Oh yes?"

"This is for your ears only."

"Understood. My lips are sealed."

"They are re-routing the *SS Mont Blanc.*"

"*Mont Blanc*?"

"Yes, a French vessel bound for Bordeaux. Re-routed to us because she is too slow to join the convoy about to leave New York."

"So, she will join our slower convoy?"

"Yes," said the Admiral, "that's the idea."

"Shouldn't be too much of a problem. We'll just have to fit her in."

"There's one more thing, Murray. I debated with myself whether to tell you. The Admiralty told me to keep it under wraps, but I felt you ought to know."

"Know what, Admiral?"

"She is loaded to the gunwales with high explosives."

"Christ!"

"A full load of TNT, guncotton, Benzol, picric acid, and God knows what else."

"The Admiralty authorized this?"

"Apparently so. Martinson didn't go into details, and it wasn't my place to ask."

"No, of course not. Although it does make one wonder about what some of our betters in London can be thinking, unleashing such a target onto the open seas."

The admiral coughed deliberately. He could not encourage such mutinous thinking, no matter how justified it might be. "You'd best keep observations like that to yourself, Murray. But the long and the short of it is that we will have to watch her very carefully indeed when she gets here."

"Duly noted, sir."

"I am guessing that our next convoy will be the largest ever to leave Halifax for Britain. What is your best estimate for departure?"

"At least a week, sir, maybe ten days."

"Hmm. Is the congestion causing any particular problems?"

"The same old problems, but much worse. Some of the pilots are barely competent, in my judgment, and others can be careless."

"The damn thing is they are out of our jurisdiction, so there's not a hell of a lot we can do about it. They've got it all locked up—the best trade union I ever heard of. Do they have a leader, or anyone among them who is highly sensible and trustworthy? Someone we can have a word with to stress the potential for trouble."

"The best man is Francis Mackey. He is very good and the others seem to look up to him. If you would like, I can arrange a meeting with him."

"Excellent. Let's do that. Of course, he can't be told about the nature of *Mont Blanc*'s cargo."

"No, Admiral."

The admiral gathered up the charts and rolled them into their cases. "You'll stay and have a bite with us, won't you, Murray?"

"Thank you, Admiral. That's the best offer I've had all day."

~

In the dining room, the admiral, Mrs. Chambers, Mrs. Hutchison, Nigel Gilchrist, William and Murray were seated around the table. Marcus had eaten earlier and gone to bed. Gilchrist and Chambers were in dress uniform, Murray in service uniform, and William in his cadet's outfit.

The cutlery and glasses gleamed and twinkled in

the light from the candles and the fire in the big grate at the end of the room. There was no food present as yet; only wine which was being circulated clockwise or "port to port".

There were two conspicuously empty chairs at the table, about which the admiral and his wife seemed nervous, Chambers frequently consulting his watch. Cameron, the butler, stood impassively to one side, apparently looking at the ceiling.

"I do apologize for keeping you waiting, Dorothea and Commander Murray." Mrs. Chambers said. "It really is too bad. They are already forty minutes late."

"Damnit, we'll start without them," said the admiral. "If they can't be here on time, it is their lookout. Cameron, you may start serving right away."

As the butler started to move towards the kitchen, a commotion in the hallway indicated that the strays had returned at last.

"Give it five more minutes, Cameron," said Mrs. Chambers.

"Very good, Madame."

Soon, the doors were flung open and Emma and Gabriel emerged, flushed, breathless and giggling.

"Where the devil have you been, Emma? Have you any idea what time it is?"

"Sorry, Uncle," said Emma contritely.

"I'm sure the delay was not Miss Emma's fault, Admiral," said Gilchrist. "I'm sure she would have been on time if she hadn't been prevented."

The admiral turned and gave him a withering glare. Glichrist coughed self-consciously and looked down at the table.

"I apologize, sir," said Gabriel. "We had a bit of trouble with the engine and had to make a forced landing. The base commander called me in to report."

"Good Heavens!" Mrs. Chambers cried, "A forced landing! Are you alright, Emma?"

"Yes, quite alright, thank you, Aunt."

"Mordie, you are to forbid her ever to go up in that aeroplane again!"

"Alright, alright! We can hear the excuses later. You're here now. For God's sake, sit down before we all starve to death. Cameron, serve immediately!"

9

The next morning, December 1, a Halifax tram car turned the corner of the snow-packed street and skidded to a halt. A number of muffled and shivering passengers alighted and hurriedly dispersed to commercial establishments in the vicinity.

One of these was Emma, who carefully picked her way across the street and made for a row of modest but solid houses, mostly of a weathered brown-gray in colour, although a few of them had been painted in patriotic red, white and blue. At the corner house, Emma stopped and knocked on the door.

After a minute or two, it was opened by Lillian Mackey, a buxom, handsome woman in her early forties, with reddish hair and a florid face. "Oh, there you are, Miss Emma. She won't be long. Come on in."

At that moment, Lillian's sister, Theresa Wrayton, pushed past her and joined Emma on the sidewalk. Theresa was the youngest of a large family, and therefore was almost 15 years younger than Lillian, with whom she had boarded since their parents passed away. She was a teacher of youngsters at Richmond School, not far from the factory where Emma worked. The two had taken to accompanying each other in the mornings and, sometimes, to town in the evening to entertainments, not all of which Mrs. Mackey or Mrs. Chambers would have considered "suitable".

"I'm ready, Lillian! Let's go, 'Em."

The two linked arms and hurried up the street, laughing as they went.

"How's that handsome Yankee of yours, Em?"

"Wonderful, thank you."

"Are you seeing him tonight?"

"Just try and stop me!"

Lillian watched them disappear around a corner, remembering what it was like to be their age; happy and free. Not that she was wholly dissatisfied with married life with Frank, or the five children, but life had certainly been a lot less onerous and a good deal more light-hearted when she was single.

She sighed and looked at her red hands, recalling how white and delicate they had once been. She was very pretty when she was young, and thought she was quite a catch, being keenly sought after, although obviously not by any man from the gentry or mercantile classes.

Just why she had chosen the serious, halting Francis was something of a mystery, as there were many other more handsome suitors. She supposed it had been that he was "steady" and had good prospects working at the port.

The years had borne out this supposition and she acknowledged she had been as well provided for as most, and better than some, of the other girls who were her youthful companions.

But, she realized, there was nothing to be gained by dwelling on the past. It was laundry day, and she had mountains of linen to boil in the old copper cauldron in the back shed.

~

That evening it was already darkening when, wrapped in layers of heavy winter clothing, Emma and Gabriel struggled up Citadel Hill, Halifax's chief landmark, which, as Fort George, was built in 1749 and dominated the city's skyline. They clung to each other as the bitter wind whipped around them. Breathless, they reached the top, turned and looked back at the harbour.

By the setting sun they could just discern as many as thirty or forty ships, of all shapes and sizes riding at anchor, all their lights extinguished for security reasons. It was an impressive, but eerie sight. The warships, in particular, looked like gray, sleeping giants which might soon be awakened, and rise in their wrath against the Hun.

"Will you love me forever and ever?" Emma entreated. "Promise me you will."

"Forever is a long time, Emma. I don't know if I can promise that far ahead. I will promise to love you until I can get my hands on your uncle's money," Gabriel answered with a cackling laugh and ran away down the hill.

"You're a rotten brute, Gabriel Hanson. A rotten brute!"

~

In New York, it was a little lighter, but darkness was gathering fast. City lights cast a glow for miles in every direction and the Statue of Liberty maintained a stern vigil over the multitude of ships filling the sea lanes.

While a large concentration of vessels was moving directly into the Atlantic, at the periphery of the activity a shabby, gray freighter was beginning her lonely voyage in another direction. At a speed of no more than three knots, *Mont Blanc* nosed its sluggish way up the south side of Long Island, heading for Nantucket, where she would take a northerly bearing for Portsmouth, thence easterly for Clark's Harbour in Nova Scotia, from where she would finally creep up the shore to Halifax.

On the very dimly lit bridge, Captain Le Medec and Levesque stood watching Glotin at the helm. Normally a departure would be the occasion for high spirits, for gossip, even jokes; but tonight a grim silence prevailed.

Looking from the bridge out over the bow they could see the new cargo which had been added just before they sailed. Stacked three and four high, supported by retaining boards and lashed down with ropes, were hundreds of large metal barrels. They faintly gleamed like some kind of sinister, lurking reptiles.

Jeremy Akerman

10

Early the following evening, the light had already faded but, despite the fact that night was descending, Halifax harbour was still alive with activity.

Welders were still at work on two submarines at Pier One, the sparks from their torches creating an eerie glow. At Pier Nine, the British vessel *Calonne* was preparing its hold for a load of horses destined for the Western Front. Britain's *Curaca* was engaged in a similar activity at Pier Eight.

The Canadian ship *Cartier* was starting to take on Cape Breton coal at Jetty Three. Also at Jetty Three was a Canadian minesweeper PV-V undergoing a refit. Norway's *Hovland* was having repairs done at the wharf dry dock, as was Canada's coal carrier *J.W.Mckee*. They were joined there by *USS Old Colony,* which was having her boiler fixed.

Mackey's little pilot boat found a place to snuggle into at the Richmond dock. He jumped out, made her fast, stood up and stretched. He had been at work since five-thirty that morning and was exhausted in mind and body. He looked up through the heavily falling snow as a bitter wind assailed him.

A mile away, up the hill, he could see faint lights twinkling, among them, he thought, the oil lamp in his own kitchen.

~

The Mackeys' kitchen was fairly large, but basic, with painted walls, plain functional furniture, and cheap oilcloth on the floor. At one end, above the sink, was a good-sized window which overlooked the harbour.

Near the stove sat Lillian, gently rocking in a big chair. Her children, all in their nightwear, sat around her, some on stools and others on the floor. At a table against the opposite wall, Theresa was marking her students' papers.

"Have you finished marking them tests yet, Theresa? I'll be needing the table as soon as the children go to bed."

"I won't be long, Lillian. Lord, there's an awful pile of them yet to do. My class is almost twice the size it was when I started teaching."

"It's the war. All the new people moving into the city. A lot of our neighbours are renting their front rooms to newcomers. Imagine how we'd be if we had to do that!"

"All eight of us confined to the kitchen wouldn't be much fun. Least of all for Frank!"

They all looked up when they heard the sound of stomping and foot scraping at the back door. When it opened, a gust of cold wind whistled through the passage, blowing snow into the room. A tired and cranky, white-covered Mackey entered.

"For the love of God, shut the door, Frank, or we'll all freeze to death!" Lillian shouted.

As Mackey closed and bolted the door, the children ran to him, grabbing his legs and all shouting at the same time.

"Let your father get out of his outdoor clothes before you go pestering him," said Lillian.

Still chattering, the children retreated as Mackey laboriously shed his layers of winter clothing, which he hung up on hooks on the back of the door. Muttering, he brushed the snow from his coat. He walked into the kitchen, appropriated the rocking chair and, with a long sigh, stiffly sat down.

The two younger children immediately climbed onto his lap.

"Well, Lilly. How's it been with you today?"

"Pretty good, Frank, although with the war going on so long, things is harder to get in the stores. Some days I wonder how I can even put a meal on the table."

"And it'll be going on a lot longer, I bet," Mackey said with conviction. "Them as told us 'it will all be over by Christmas' were talking through their asses."

"Frank, please! Not in front of the kids."

"Well, it makes me sick. They said that in 1914, for God's sake. They were only four years out! I can't see any end to it, not from where I'm sitting. I shouldn't be surprised if it goes on for another two or three years."

"Lord! Don't be saying that! In two or three years' time we'd be lucky to find a bun of bread anywhere in the city."

"Well, I sure hope you've got some for us tonight. And more than bread, too!"

"Yes, I've got stew, and bread. It'll be on the table as soon as these scallywags goes to bed. Go on, children! Scoot! Up them stairs right away. Your father is beat and needs some peace."

She shooed them out of the room, then turned back to her husband. "Lord, Frank, you do look all in. I never seen your eyes looking so red before."

Mackey rubbed his eyes and ran his hands over his head. He turned to his sister-in-law. "Sorry, Theresa. We've been ignoring you all this time. How are you doing?"

"Good, Frank. Just finishing up some marking, then I'll lay the table. I'm going out with Emma later."

"And tomorrow night, too," said Lillian. "Are you sure all this gallivanting every night is good for you?"

"I'm young, I'm free! When I get tired I'll stay in and rest."

"Well, it sure sounds like a good plan to me. I wish I could go with you," said Mackey.

"As if!" Lillian hooted. "I can just see you doing a jig in your state!"

"It's the long hours as are getting to me. I never worked so many shifts before. There's so many ships a-coming and a-going. It will be murder when the convoy ships out."

"There's not enough pilots. That's the trouble," said Theresa, "You should be training some young fellows to ease the strain on you."

"That's what you think, young lady. If we did that there wouldn't be enough work to go around when the port slacks off."

"Come on, Theresa, move yourself!" said Lillian, bearing in a huge pot of deliciously-smelling stew and plonking it on the table. "Sit up, Frank, and get this down you afore you falls asleep!"

Jeremy Akerman

11

The following evening, December 3, Gabriel stood on a street corner, pulling his uniform around him to keep out the cold. Even his Navy greatcoat did little to improve his comfort. His breath swirled about his reddened face. He needed to get moving and keep moving if he was to warm up.

Pedestrians struggled along the street on their way home from work. Some were laden with parcels of goods bought from the shops. Drawn by a pair of rather ill-kept Clydesdales, a brewer's dray clattered by.

Then, arm in arm and laughing boisterously, Emma and Theresa came cavorting towards him. When they reached Gabriel, they grabbed his arms and whirled him around.

"Hello Gabe," said Emma. "We were just talking about you."

"What were you saying?"

"Oh, this and that," said Theresa.

"Well, whatever it was, can we please get out of

this cold? Don't forget I've been hanging around waiting for you two for ages."

"Alright. Follow me!" Theresa said, skipping away down the street.

"Where is she taking us? And what kind of mischief are you getting us into?"

"I guess we'll soon find out."

"I could lose my commission if involves anything illegal," said Gabriel,

Theresa turned into a darkened alleyway and knocked at a dirty, battered door. They were admitted by a shifty-looking man and ushered down into a basement from which loud strains of Celtic music rose to meet them.

"Jesus!" cursed Gabriel. "This is a blind pig!"

"Yes, I expect it is," Emma replied.

This made Gabriel uncomfortable because it placed him in a delicate position. In 1910, Nova Scotia had passed the Temperance Act, enforcing prohibition of alcoholic beverages in Nova Scotia except the City of Halifax, but in 1916 the law was extended to the capital, and while liquor could be legally produced in Canada and exported from Canadian ports, it could not be sold or consumed in the country.

In Gabriel's own country, after the United States entered earlier that year, President Wilson had instituted a temporary wartime prohibition on alcohol in order to save grain for producing food. Congress then drafted the 18th Amendment, which banned the manufacture, transportation and sale of intoxicating liquors, and submitted it to the states for ratification. So, a United States citizen who consumed liquor was guilty whichever way the matter was considered.

Gabriel hoped they would not meet anyone here who knew him and, if they did, that it would be a fellow officer who could not report him without incriminating himself.

The dance floor reverberated with working-class men and women swinging each other about in a wild frenzy. In a corner a bodhrán player, a mandolinist, two fiddlers and a spoon player furiously stomped out *Turkey in the Straw* and *The Milkmaids of Blantyre*. Her red hair flying, Theresa laughed and spun around as she clutched a good-looking dock worker.

Where they managed to get seats near the dance floor, Emma and Gabriel indicated their approval by thumping the table.

The band moved into *Loch Lomond* and then *Rose of Tralee*, Theresa and her partner slowly circling the room.

"She's really wild, isn't she?"

"They call her the Devil's child," said Emma with a

laugh.

They paid the shifty man for the rough whisky which he put in front of them, and warily sniffed the glasses. Emma wrinkled up her nose and declined to sample the beverage. Gabriel took a swig and grimaced.

Emma took his hand and for some minutes they watched the dancing, swaying to the music.

"Have you told your aunt and uncle yet?"

"Told them what?"

"You know. Told them that I have asked you to marry me and that you agreed."

"Oh that." She smiled at him. "Not yet. They are British, you know."

"So are you."

"We don't do these things that way they are done in America."

She paused and looked at him. The disappointment on his face was sufficient to melt her resolve to wait. "Oh, alright. Why don't we tell them together? Come over tomorrow night. We can do it then."

"Tomorrow? Damn! I can't. I have to fly a mission and I don't know what time I'll get back. We're intensifying reconnaissance for U-boats. I'm so sorry, Em."

"Maybe the next day."

"Yes, maybe that will work."

Theresa's red hair again flew past them as the band played *Planxty Johnson*, an ancient tune written by the blind harper Turlough O'Carolan at the turn of the seventeenth century. Its beautiful, though somehow sad, rhythms matched their mood.

Jeremy Akerman

12

The sky was clear, but the sun had yet to climb over the treetops on the Dartmouth side of the harbour. The United States Naval base was cold and dark. It was Tuesday, December 4.

Pilots were standing around, smoking as they watched their ground crews trundle their seaplanes down the rollers towards the water. There were four planes this morning, an already-outdated Burgess-Dunne Hydro being kept behind for repairs. Gabriel's Curtis H2SL, two Curtis H12s, and a Curtis H-16 each were painted with white star centred in a blue circle and a red disc within the star.

The American aircraft industry had come a long way in a very short time. When the U.S. declared war on the German Empire, its armed forces had only 54 aircraft of all descriptions, fewer than 50 flying officers and just over 200 ratings assigned to naval and Marine airplanes.

Rapidly, aircraft of many types entered production, and thousands of new aviators, ground officers, mechanics, and technical specialists came into being. The U.S. Army opened Love Field in Dallas as a flight training base, and the Naval Aircraft Factory was established in Philadelphia. Now, the navy's flyers were actively engaged in France, the Azores and Canada, as well as regularly patrolling the coasts of the United States.

In a shed behind Gabriel and his colleagues, under a heavily armed guard, lurked the Navy's new "flying bomb", manufactured by the Curtiss Company, which had been shipped from its testing ground on Long Island, New York. The designers intended the flying bomb—also called an aerial torpedo—to carry 1,000 pounds of explosives, with a range of 50 miles and a top speed of 90 miles per hour. It was all very "hush hush". Gabriel and his colleagues were told nothing about it, and they asked no questions.

The men clambered into a small dinghy and were ferried out to where their aircraft had been towed. The other pilots were taking their 'spotters' with them, men who occupied the nose seats and watched out for submarines; but as his plane was still suspected of problems in cold weather and additional weight would not be advantageous, Gabriel had been instructed to fly this mission on his own.

He hauled himself into the cockpit and, at a sign from the commanding officer, started the engine. As it roared into life, he gave the thumbs-up signal to the shore crew, then turned his craft and headed for the open sea.

Moving rapidly, he skimmed the plane over the surface and then rose up into the sky. The sun was also now fully up as he headed along the eastern shore.

Away to his right he noticed an old whaler, about 500 feet long and of approximately 5000 tons, making its way towards the harbour. He peeled away to take a closer look, and when he got nearer saw she was flying the Norwegian flag and had 'Belgian Relief' painted on the side of her hull.

For fun, he buzzed the bridge, waved to the helmsman, then flew on.

~

Rear Admiral Chambers' office in Naval Command was a long, airy room lit by the large windows overlooking the harbour. He sat at his desk, flanked by Nigel Gilchrist and Commander Murray.

Across the desk from them sat three men: Captain Garnett and Commander Triggs of the HMS *Highflyer*, and Francis Mackey. The naval officers seemed uneasy in the admiral's presence, but Mackey was nonchalantly lounging in an armchair.

"I hope you understand, Admiral," said Mackey forcefully, "that I don't report to you or to Commander Murray. I don't work for the British Navy."

"Oh yes, we're quite aware of that, Mr. Mackey. I asked you here—on an informal basis—because we need your help."

"How? What do you need?"

"Murray, you're closest to the problem. You put Mr. Mackey in the picture."

"Certainly, sir. You know yourself, Mr. Mackey, that the situation in the port is getting out of hand. The sheer number of vessels is bound to create some confusion. Isn't that so, Garnett?"

"Yes. From *Highflyer*," said Garnett, "Commander Triggs and I have witnessed a number of worrying incidents just in the past few days—"

"I don't like being ganged up on," Mackey interrupted. "You Brits have got me outnumbered."

"It is not like that, I assure you," said the Admiral, "and it is because we have great respect for you that we asked you to come and help us."

"Alright." Mackey was placated. "Go on."

"I think you'd find it hard to deny that all the pilots are overworked," said Murray, "and that, well, some of them are—shall we say—less than perfect."

"So?" Mackey could not restrain a slight grin.

"The next few days are crucial," the admiral put in,

"until the convoy leaves. If you could try to impress upon your colleagues the necessity of taking extra precautions, it would be greatly appreciated."

"I don't like hearing my guys criticized by you—or anyone else, but I take your point and I'll see what I can do. No promises, mind."

"No, of course not." The admiral rose. "Mr. Mackey, thank you so much for coming."

~

Within a few hours, intelligence of the admiral's meeting, and of its nature, had reached the ears of Sydney Mewburn, the new federal Minister of Militia and Defence. It is a matter for speculation as to which of the meeting's participants advised the minister, but he received the information with concern and annoyance.

Like his predecessors, Sam Hughes and Albert Kemp, Mewburn chafed under the yoke of the situation at Halifax whereby responsibility was divided, with local, British and Canadian authorities each having their fingers in what he saw as a rather messy pie.

"Something must be done about this," he told his deputy minister, Eugene Fiset. "Not least because we are dealing with the Prime Minister's own constituency."

Mewburn was 54, with wavy grey hair, a drooping moustache and sleepy eyes. He represented Hamilton East in the Canadian parliament, a constituency which was some 1200 miles from the sea. He had taken office only a month ago, and was anxious to make his mark and please his leader.

"The entire port of Halifax and all its functions should be under the federal government. It only makes sense."

"I agree, Minister," said Fiset obsequiously, "and it could be done, if you had the will to do it." He handed the minister a small booklet containing an Act of Parliament passed in August of 1914.

"The War Measures Act! Yes I know all about that."

He did indeed. The Act gave sweeping powers to the cabinet, allowing it to bypass parliament. Under the Act, the government could censor and suppress communications and arrest, detain and deport people without charge or trial. It could control transport, trade and manufacturing, and seize private property. People could be arrested and imprisoned for their political beliefs. And it made the declaration of Martial Law easy.

"But to seize the entire port of Halifax would not be acceptable to the Prime Minister's constituents unless there were a solid, overriding reason," said

Mewburn. "If we could find that reason, we could do it."

"Maybe that reason will come along of its own accord," said Fiset in an oracular tone. "*Peut-être Le Bon Dieu fournira.*"

"Well, I wish he would do it sooner rather than later," Mewburn said gruffly.

~

At the Naval Academy, William sat in the second row from the back. It was a large room, lit by three big windows looking out over the water. Some fifteen cadets were intently listening to an instructor, who paced back and forth in front of a blackboard.

"Article 25 of the 'Regulations for Preventing Collisions at Sea'. Who can cite it? Anybody?"

The instructor's invitation elicited only silence from his class.

"Come on! Wilcox? Benson? MacQueen?"

Each boy glumly shook his head as he was called.

"Nobody! Very well, write this down, all of you. 'In narrow channels every steam vessel shall, when it is safe and practicable, keep to the side of the fairway or mid-channel which lies on the starboard side of such vessel'."

"It's awfully confusing sir," said young Wilcox.

"Not the language I would have chosen, but the King's English nonetheless. Who can tell me what it means? Chambers, how about you?"

"Yes sir," said William, rising nervously. "Does it mean that if there are two ships they each must pass on their port side?"

"Yes indeed! Port to port. Left bow to left bow. Engrave it in your memories."

The light was starting to fade somewhat and the pupils were getting restless.

"Settle down!" commanded the instructor. "It's not time to go home yet."

There was a loud communal groan from the boys. Each had hoped the time was further advanced, but none had pocket watches, and the instructor had covered the classroom clock with the blackboard.

"Right! Attention, please. Now then, two blasts on a ship's whistle means...what, MacQueen?"

"Um, does it mean stop, sir?"

"Foolish boy. No it does not. Benson?"

"Does it mean 'I am altering my course to port'?"

"Well done! Or....what else could it mean."

William's hand went up.

"Yes, Chambers?"

"It means 'I am on the right course and intend to stay on it'."

"Absolutely right. Very important. We'll make sailors of you yet."

"Please, can we go now, sir?" asked a tiny boy named Anstruther.

"Yes, alright. There are still four minutes remaining, but on this occasion, I shall let you go."

There was a loud scramble as the boys fought to grab their schoolbags, squeeze out of the classroom and charge out into the yard. They were free…until tomorrow.

Jeremy Akerman

13

Gabriel scoured the ocean surface for signs of U-boat movement. To date, there had been few encounters within a hundred miles of shore, but reports had circulated of a recent visit by a newer and bigger German submarine. Details were scanty, but apparently "The Ghost", as it had been dubbed, had further range than the previous generation of U-boats, and carried more and bigger torpedoes.

He thought he spied something off his starboard wing and banked down to take a closer look. As the plane lost altitude, the engine gave a sputter and went into a perceptible rocking. Gabriel rapped his gauges, shrugged and resumed the northeast course he had been previously pursuing.

A few miles further on the plane starting jerking strongly, its engine revolutions seeming to alternate between high and low. Gabriel was being thrust forward, then thrown back.

A thick blanket of fog had rolled in from the Atlantic, limiting visibility. Through gaps in the fog, far below, he could see a small fishing village down on the shoreline, its weathered shacks beaten and gray by a harsh winter environment.

As the jerking and sputtering increased, he tapped his gauges again, then, with great difficulty, extracted the flight map from his tunic. The paper flapped furiously in the wind and it was hard to see anything, but he could just figure out that he was now much too far from the base to limp home.

He banked again as gently as he could, but the engine suddenly revved into a whine and started to spin. Gabriel frantically fought with the flight stick, trying to regain control, but it was no good. The Curtis stalled and started to drop like a stone towards the icy waters below.

The ocean loomed and, with a huge splash, nose first, the plane hit the sea, slamming Gabriel against the dashboard. The impact of the crash snapped off the plane's tail section, which floated away on the waves, then tore back the wings. Water poured through many ruptures in the fuselage.

As sheets of fog rolled in across the waves, the waterlogged, skeletal remains of the Curtis slowly sank lower into the water.

The water was now around Gabriel's waist as the cockpit was flooding. He was lacerated, bruised, dazed and freezing. As far as he could tell no bones had been broken, but his skin was turning blue.

He found it very difficult to move, but with sheer determination he unbuckled his harness, pushed himself free of the wreckage and grabbed one of the wing flaps which had come loose. Pushing off with his feet, and using the flap as a flotation device, he paddled towards the shore. A large wave slammed into him and he was temporarily completely submerged. Gabriel, gasping and spluttering, continued to paddle weakly.

About half an hour later, the fog had rolled in thicker than ever. Gabriel, his strength gone and his life waning, could no longer grip the wing flap and, as his arm slipped away from his support, he slid into the sea.

He knew he was drowning, dying, but he also knew there was nothing he could do about it. Visions of Emma, his lovely, never-to-be-seen-again Emma, came to him as he drifted into unconsciousness.

Suddenly, a sturdy hand grasped his wrist and hauled him bodily over the side of a black and white Cape Island fishing boat.

Harold Wambolt thought Gabriel was dead for certain, but decided to take him ashore and report the body to the authorities. The boy's uniform was soaking wet, so was not easy to identify, so he might have been a German.

As he turned the boat and made for the distant wharf, his passenger groaned.

Harold put a boot on him, and slid the shotgun from its place behind the wheel. "You aint goin' nowhere. You just lie still 'till I gets you ashore. Then we'll see who you are, mister."

A large, gray, weather-beaten house stood facing the ocean only yards from the water's edge. The yard, containing a few scratching chickens, bales of netting, and lobster traps waiting to be repaired, was a mess of frozen mud and dirty snow.

Standing expectantly in the yard was Doris Wambolt, a woman in her early fifties, watching her husband bring his boat alongside the wharf. Their son, Hector, ran down from the house to meet his father and, taking the ropes thrown to him, made fast the boat.

They managed to heave Gabriel's body out of the vessel and on to the planks. Hector threw a heavy blanket over him and, one at each end, they picked him up and carried him up to the house.

"What you got there Harold, a giant haddock?" Doris called.

"Some flyer feller. All in by the looks of him. Better get another blanket, Doris. Where'll we put him?"

"Jesus! Best put him on the couch in the best room, I guess. Did he drop out of the sky?"

"Pretty much. His airyplane is all smashed up and sunk by now, I reckon. Come on, Hector, let's get him inside."

"Wait till I opens the door for you. Don't be handling him like he's a sack of spuds!"

"Alright, woman. Why don't you fetch out that bottle of rum I got stashed away. I'll give him a snort of that. I reckon he's gonna need some reviving. And put on a pot of soup, too. He'll need that later."

Doris disappeared into the house, from where she could be heard banging around in kitchen cupboards. Harold and Hector bundled Gabriel into the front, 'best' room, which was only marginally better furnished than the other rooms, and installed him on the couch.

Watching from the doorway was daughter Margaret, who had been brought downstairs by all the commotion. She was an outstandingly attractive young brunette in her early twenties, with an angelic face and a mind filled with romantic notions.

"Dad, Hector, for the love of God, you can't leave him wrapped up like that," she said. "He's soaking wet, for one thing, and maybe he's got cuts and such as should be taken care of."

"Alright, we'll leave him to you," said Harold. "But listen now, Margaret..."

"What?"

"You can only be alone with him so long as he's unconscious or until we knows more about him."

"Oh, alright, Dad."

Margaret lit a fire in the grate and got it going, and then fetched more blankets and a flannel nightgown of her father's. Then she gingerly removed the first blankets, which were mostly wet by now, and dumped them in the washhouse.

She carefully removed Gabriel's clothes, piece by piece, until he was naked. She gasped when she saw the large cuts and enormous bruises on his torso, but bathed them gently with a sponge and treated them with the necessary dressings and salves. Gabriel grunted when she applied iodine to his cuts, but relapsed into unconsciousness.

As softly as she could, she drew the nightshirt over his head, manoeuvred his arms through the holes, then eased it under his buttocks and pulled it down around his legs. Then she drew the fresh blankets about him and tucked them in.

"Look at you, mister," she said quietly. "I don't know who you are. If you ain't one of them Germans, I got plans for you."

The Wambolts rigged up a spare bed and moved it closer to the woodstove, which burned fiercely in the centre of the main downstairs room. Gabriel lay motionless under his blankets as a kettle and a large pot both bubbled and whistled on the stove.

At the sink, Doris was peeling potatoes and turnips. Hector and Harold were dragging wood across the yard from the big pile at the side of the house. Margaret sat beside Gabriel's bed, dabbing his forehead with a damp cloth.

The men came in and stacked the firewood by the stove, removed their boots and flopped down in two cheap cane chairs.

"Who is he, Dad?" Margaret asked.

"As far as I can tell, he's one of them American flyers from down Baker's Point," said Harold, getting up to feed another log to the stove. "I had a look at his uniform and the badge or whatever you calls it is American."

"An areoplane man!" Margaret said, stroking Gabriel's hair.

"I don't understand why anyone would want to go flying up there in a big piece of wood. Makes no sense to me," said Hector.

"He fell right out of the sky and landed here," Margaret said.

"Now don't go getting fancy romantic ideas, our Margaret. As soon as he's on his feet, you keep your distance!" said Harold. "How's that soup coming along, Doris?"

"Won't be long. Time for you and Heckie to wash

your hands."

Margaret looked down at her patient, and spoke softly to herself. "Look how peaceful he is. He's some beautiful. It's like he was sent here special."

14

Emma poked her head round the classroom door at Richmond School and saw Theresa cleaning off the blackboard. Time was wasting and she was impatient.

"Come on, Theresa! Don't hang about!"

"Alright, alright. I'll be with you in a minute. What's the big rush?"

"I need your help this evening. Very special help."

Theresa clapped the board cleaners together, creating cloud of chalk dust, then replaced them on the ledge. "You are being very mysterious," she said. "Out with it. Tell me what you want."

"I want you to help me choose a wedding dress!"

"Gracious! What has brought this on?"

"We decided we want to get married, so we will."

"Alright, Mrs Hanson-to-be. Let's go."

"But hurry. Nation and Shewan's is only open until seven tonight. If we have to come back on Saturday, the best dresses might have been sold."

Half an hour later, they clambered down from a

trolley bus and stood outside one of the large windows of Nation and Shewan, the other being devoted to men's wear. Theresa pointed to the most old-fashioned, fussy dresses, while Emma drew her attention to the sleeker, more modern models.

"What is the matter with you, Theresa? You want me to look like your grandmother, but I want to look like Mary Pickford!"

"I think you should try to look like Queen Mary," said Theresa slyly. "Be dignified."

"Be throttled by sixteen rows of pearls! And have an enormous bosom trapped in ten pounds of lace and a blue sash. I don't think so!"

"No, you couldn't carry it off with your little bosoms. Let's go in. You never know, you might find something."

Giggling, they opened the door and went into what seemed like a wonderland of luxury and enticement.

It was almost closing time before they had found a dress on which they and the saleslady could all agree. Strangely, it was an old-fashioned dress after all, but was not at all fussy, and its simplicity was what attracted them to it. It was in a style which had been popular in the last century, with a wide skirt, a square neckline, and pointed waist.

The saleslady told them the dress was designed

by Lucy Duff Gordon in New York, and was special because of its quarter-length close over-sleeves, stomacher, 'vee' waistline and plain lace underskirt. The price made them gasp, but Emma was sure she could raise the money, especially if she were extra nice to her uncle.

The saleslady pinned a silver card to the dress, indicating that it was provisionally sold to Miss Emma Chambers.

"They won't keep that dress for you forever, you know," said Theresa as they tripped along the street to get a bus back to the north end and the admiral's house. "You're going to have to bite the bullet pretty soon."

"I know—"

"And that means breaking the news to the dragons."

"Don't you dare speak of my aunt and uncle like that. And certainly not when you meet them. Dragons, indeed!"

"But, Em, you have to do it soon. If only to keep the dress."

"I've already decided, I think, that I'll do it later tonight. But here's our bus. When we get there, you must come in and meet 'the dragons'. You never know, you might like them."

"You're joking! They don't want to meet the likes

of me. They're the mucky-mucks and I am as common as dirt."

"I wish you wouldn't talk that way. Anyone would think you were one of those Russian revolutionaries."

"We'll soon find out. But I bet they won't approve. They won't think I am 'suitable'."

Some hours later Emma was sitting in her bedroom, which was luxurious by the standards of common people. While she appreciated the space and amenities, secretly she would have preferred to be back in the small, cozy room in her late father's house in the west of England.

Expecting a scene, she hugged her knees and braced herself. Her aunt sat upright in a nearby easy chair.

"You didn't like her, did you?"

"I neither liked her, nor disliked her," said Mrs. Chambers primly. "You are perfectly able to choose your own friends. You know, I wouldn't dream of trying to dictate to you."

"But...?"

"Please don't be impertinent. I was about to say that you can spend as much time as you like with Miss Wrayton. But it would be better if you didn't bring her here."

"Is she not 'suitable'?"

"Since you mention it, she is not. Miss Wrayton may have many attributes, but clearly discretion is not among them. The admiral has all manner of important people coming to the house and he cannot afford to offend any of them. Besides which, much of the discussion in this house is about the war, and what is said here is of a confidential nature and must stay here."

"I'm sorry if I've displeased you, Aunt."

"Emma, dear, I am not displeased with you."

"Well, I fear you will be when you hear what I have to say next."

"And what is that?"

"Gabriel and I are pledged to be married"

Mrs. Chambers was clearly shocked, but managed to compose herself and not reveal her true feelings. "Well, you are of age, Emma, and may marry whomever you choose. Unless your choice was utterly unthinkable, I am sure your uncle will give you away and will help you with money as best his means allow."

"And what about you, Auntie?"

Mrs. Chambers was about to speak when there was a knock on the door.

"Yes, come in!" said Emma.

The admiral put his head round the door and gingerly put a foot into the room. "Please excuse me,

Emma, my dear, I have some rather rotten news. I have just had a call from Gabriel's Commanding Officer. His plane has not returned to base. I am afraid he is missing."

"Is that all we know, Mordie?"

"Well…no. Reconnaissance has seen some wreckage in the sea. They think it is his plane."

Wailing like a lost animal, Emma ran to her aunt and buried her face in her lap.

~

Some eighty-five miles to the northeast, at the Wambolt house, Gabriel lay next to the stove which, even at this late hour, had been kept burning brightly. The room was lit by the glow of the stove and by a single candle on the table. Gabriel was still not conscious, but his face had gained colour and looked much better for the constant care Margaret had been providing.

She bent over and kissed his forehead. "I love you, aeroplane man."

She stood up and blew out the candle.

15

The sun had not yet risen, but the slightly lightning sky promised that sunrise was not far off. It was Wednesday, December 5, 1917.

Still far out at sea, a dirty tramp steamer was slowly chugging towards the port of Halifax. She was fully loaded, very low in the water and was sluggish despite being under full steam. She moved through the water as if she were dragging her chequered past behind her. This was *Mont Blanc*, which had left New York some days ago

She was a cargo ship built in Middlesbrough, England, in 1899 for the French shipping company, Société Générale de Transport Maritime. A typical three-islander, she was steel-hulled, with a fo'c's'le, bridge and poop, an economical construction which was common in tramps in the nineteenth and early twentieth centuries. Originally registered in Marseilles, she was bought in 1906 by M. Anquetil, who re-registered her in Rouen. In 1915 she passed to another Rouen ship-owner called Gaston Petit. Later that year, she was purchased by the Compagnie Générale Transatlantique, which registered her in Saint-Nazaire, at the mouth of the Loire on France's west coast.

Her bridge was lit with a pale yellow glow which revealed Levesque at the helm and Le Medec standing behind and to one side of him. Glotin was nearby, studying the charts. They were behind time, their passage having been retarded due to the extraordinary weight she was carrying.

However, there was nothing anyone could to accelerate their progress.

~

About the same time as *Mont Blanc* was making her weary and solemn way to Halifax, Francis Mackey held a meeting with the other port pilots. He passed on the message he had received from Admiral Chambers.

His audience that morning was hostile, to say the least.

"We don't take no orders from the likes of him," shouted Thomas Wentzell. "He's a frigging limey!"

"Who does he think he is, pushing us around?" demanded Rannie Cooper. "Nobody does that to us!"

"Calm down, boys, I'm only the messenger,"

Mackey said. "Don't be attacking me. All the man was trying to say was that we're going to be awful cramped in the harbour next week, so there's bound to be more chances for trouble."

"What were you doing meeting with that guy anyway, Frank?" Bill Hayes demanded. "How come it was only you and not the rest of us? All high and mighty, aren't you! Think you're better'n us, do you?"

"I give up," Mackey cried. "Do what you want. If there's some accident, don't be blaming me!"

He climbed down from the box on which he had been standing, pushed through the rows of men, and stalked away. He hoped that, regardless of the tone of the meeting, at least some of the pilots would think more carefully about the situation and exercise a greater degree of caution. He had done what was asked of him and could do no more. It was now in the lap of the gods.

~

The sharp, early-morning sun stabbed through the windows and illuminated a now-fully-conscious Gabriel, sitting at the kitchen table and greedily gobbling a second helping of bacon and eggs. He was covered in cuts and bruises and was clearly still weak from his ordeal.

Doris cleared away dirty dishes as Harold roamed around the room, looking for his gloves. Across from Gabriel sat Margaret, staring adoringly.

"Do you want some more tea, Gabriel?"

"It'd be a wonder if he could fit anything else in!" Doris said with a laugh.

"No, thank you, Margaret. By the way, you never told me where we are. What is this place?"

"This is Harrigan Cove," said Margaret.

"Harrigan Cove," repeated Gabriel. "That's a place I'll never forget."

"Have you seen my right glove, Doris?" Harold called from the other side of the room.

"Well, I must go," Gabriel said firmly.

"Go?" Margaret sounded almost as if she were in pain. "You ain't well enough to go anywhere. Is he, Ma?"

"I should have thought he'd need another day," said Doris, "but if he's a mind to go, there's nothing we can do about it."

"Yes, I must get back to Halifax. They'll all be worried about me. Likely, they'll think I'm dead."

"But your wounds are still not healed," Margaret insisted.

"Let the man go," said Harold. "He's going to do what he wants anyway."

"But, Dad—"

"That enough, Margaret! Put this coat on, Gabriel. I hope it fits you. It was my dead brother's coat. I'm sorry that yours is fit for nothing but the trash, what with being waterlogged and cut apart to get at your wounds."

"Thank you, Harold. Thank you, Doris, for your kindness," Gabriel said. "And thank you to the gentlest nurse a man could ever wish for. Margaret, I shall never forget what you've done for me."

Somewhat unsteadily, he put on the coat and followed Harold to the door. When he looked back, he saw that Margaret was in tears, but was a vision of loveliness in her sorrow.

Harold took him some miles in his horse and trap and let him out at the top of a hill overlooking the bay. To the south were two islands, covered in snow, which Harold said were Hog Island and Little Hog Island and, beyond them a larger island called Batiste. On the landward side all Gabriel could see was a never-ending tract of hills carpeted with snow-covered spruce.

Harold turned to the west and pointed across to a narrow road. "That there is Shier's road. They say it was named after some Irish people what come over in the 1700s. Anyway, you go down there."

"Are you sure?' Gabriel asked. "It doesn't seem very substantial and looks like it goes nowhere."

"Listen, boy, you got 70 miles to go to get to Truro, so do as I say and it'll be the shortest and best for you. Understand?"

"Yes," said Gabriel meekly.

"I don't know as where you'll spend tonight. Maybe someone will pick you up along the way."

"I sure hope so."

"After Shier's Road, carry on to Sheet Harbour, then go north until you hits the Halifax-New Glasgow Road and go to Upper Stewiacke. Then go up through Brookfield to Truro. You can get a train there."

"Isn't there a train down the shore from here to Halifax?"

"Only from Musquodoboit Harbour. You'd have to walk more'n 60 miles to get there. Then you never know how long you'd have to wait for your train. Neither is a good choice, but I'd say you'd be better off heading for Truro."

"Alright. I'll take your advice. Thanks again, Harold."

"God bless you my boy. Don't be forgettin' us."

"I won't. Never."

~

The noise coming from the Dominion Textile factory

was loud at the best of times, but in the long room which occupied the entire second floor of the building it was deafening. On each side was a row of clattering, belt-driven looms operated by women in gray work suits. Several male supervisors, and one female overseer, paced the central aisle, barking orders.

Downstairs in the office, a red-eyed Emma stared out of the window, her gaze fixed on the snow-flecked sky. A portly, well-dressed man who had been on the telephone came out of the inner office and approached her.

"Still no word, I'm sorry, Emma. I'm sure they will find him soon."

~

Many hours later, Gabriel had wearily passed through Sheet Harbour and was heading north. He found the going very heavy. In some places the snow was deep, in others thick mud was just below a fragile surface of ice. On either side of the road, which was little more than a track in places, were tall evergreen trees with clumps of snow weighing down their branches.

The forest had an air of unnatural calmness with very few birds in evidence except for the ubiquitous crows. Were they the same crows, following him, he wondered, or different crows occupying different tribal territories he entered?

He pulled his coat more tightly around him as he was now extremely cold, despite the many woolen layers the Wambolts had given him. The gloves were too small and cramped his fingers while leaving his wrists to freeze as he swung his arms.

Several miles back he had wolfed down the bread and fish they had wrapped for him in several pages of *The Eastern Chronicle* and stuffed in his coat pocket. It was almost frozen when he came to eat it, but he devoured it gratefully nonetheless.

Just as despair was starting to set in, Gabriel heard what at first sounded like the whining of an animal in pain. But when he turned around he realized it came from the creaking of the wheels of a large cart being pulled by an old, gray mare. He stood aside on the bank to let the cart go past, but when it reached him it stopped.

"Good day to you sir," said a very old, very black man, wearing a Balaclava helmet.

"Good day. I'm heading to Truro where I have to get a train."

"Well, you ain't catchin' no train any time soon if you're goin' to walk the whole way. Why don't you hop up alongside of me?"

Needing no second bidding, Gabriel climbed up and off they went.

The man's name was Jerimiah Borden, and his horse was called Delilah. In short order his benefactor had learned Gabriel's entire history and how he had come to be on a lonely road in a Nova Scotia winter.

The waning afternoon sun had given way to a leaden, overcast pall. They drove through some farming villages in which the few houses were battened down for the winter, smoke drifting from their chimneys into a rapidly darkening sky. Near the road, a man and his son were tending to some cows in a snow-blown field.

"All things come to an end," announced Jerimiah. "Just like the summer dies and turns to winter, so our lives will end and be taken up by our children. You have children, Gabriel?"

"No, but Emma and I would like to have some. We plan to be married soon."

"That is what the Good Lord put us here for. To serve him and to have our children to serve him. I see many people not living The Way and, you know, He's keepin' a tally for the final judgment."

Eventually, long after dark, Jerimiah stopped his cart by the railway station. It seemed almost deserted, but Gabriel climbed down in a cheerful mood.

"I can't thank you enough, Jerimiah. I could have been out on that road for days. Maybe I would have frozen to death had it not been for you."

"The Lord works all things for a reason, Gabriel, you remember that. God be with you, son."

As Jerimiah and Delilah clip-clopped down the street, Gabriel turned to the station, walked in and went to the ticket window, which the agent seemed to be closing for the day.

"Are there any trains to Halifax tonight, please?"

"'Fraid not" said the agent. "Next one is tomorrow morning around 7.30."

"Damn. Do you have a telephone I could use, please?"

"That's strictly against the rules. The calls are all recorded, so if I let you use it, I could get the sack."

"I wouldn't want to do that," said Gabriel.

'Tell you what," said the agent. " You could stay here for the night. If you promise not to tell anyone, you can curl up by the fire. It's still got a bit of go in it. I'll lock you in."

~

It was black as pitch when Francis Mackey's little pilot boat pulled alongside *Mont Blanc*. He made her fast, then clambered up the rope ladder they had thrown him.

On the bridge were Le Medec, Glotin and Levesque, waiting for him. Mackey shook hands with all three.

"Good night, gentlemen. I am Frank Mackey, your pilot."

"*M'excuse*, M. Mackey," said Le Medec, "but I 'ave only lil bit English and my *officiers* have less than me. Do you speak French?"

"No, sorry, Captain. I don't speak any French. Only a bit of Gaelic."

The Frenchmen looked at each other, frowning. Mackey was about to attempt to explain, when a loud ship's gun was heard. They turned to him for an explanation.

"The gun means we can't go in tonight, captain. The boom has been closed for the day. We can move in the morning."

He pointed ahead. They could just see the string of floats marking the boom of the anti-submarine net.

"*Ah, oui*. For the U-boats, yes? So we cannot go tonight. What will you do? Why not sleep on board?"

"Thanks, Captain, that's very kind of you. I accept your invitation."

"*Bon bien!* Glotin, M. Mackey can have my cabin. I

will take him down now."

Le Medec led Mackey to the surprisingly large cabin. A steward followed them to the door, awaiting orders.

"Be comfortable. You will have a café? French regulations will not allow me to offer *alcool*."

"*Obtenez de nouveaux draps pour ma couchette, Duviq*," Le Medec said to the Steward, "*et deux cafés s'il vous plaît*."

Mackey took the best available seat and stretched out. There was a tap at the door, and Glotin appeared with Commander Murray.

"Good evening, Captain. Oh, hello, Mackey."

"Evening Mr. Murray."

"*Comandeur, c'est un grand plaisir de vous connaitre*."

"Also for me, Captain." Murray perched himself on the edge on the captain's small desk. "Here are your instructions. You should proceed tomorrow on a signal from *H.M.S. Niobe*. It will probably be shortly after first light. Likely around 0715 hours. In the meantime, I have to examine the ship's manifest. Do you understand, Captain?"

Le Medec nodded. He had been expecting this. He unlocked a shiny, wooden chest, took out the pertinent papers and gave them to Murray. The commander examined them without a word.

“Thank you, Captain Le Medec. They are quite in order,” said Murray, handing the manifest to Mackey.

The pilot looked at the first page, then quickly leafed through the remaining pages. The blood drained from his face.

“Jesus Christ!” he said.

Jeremy Akerman

16

Early the next day, the ticket agent unlocked the waiting room door and let in the cold, pale, morning light. It was Thursday, December 6.

"Rise and shine, young man!" he said. "The Halifax train is due in about three quarters of an hour and pretty soon this place will be buzzing."

"Good morning to you, sir," Gabriel said. "Do you expect there'll be many passengers for this train?"

"A fair few, I reckon. I expect maybe twenty or so, going to Halifax for Christmas shopping."

"Oh yes, of course. I'd forgotten that Christmas is coming."

"I hope you had a reasonable night under the circumstances."

"Thank you. Not bad," replied Gabriel. "Although it did get a bit chilly after the fire went out."

"You'd best come and have a quick cup of tea with me, then I must be about my duties."

"Again, many thanks for your kindness. I better get a ticket before the crowd comes."

"Let's take care of that first. Then I'll put the kettle on for tea."

As it turned out, there were more people going to Halifax than the agent had predicted, and Gabriel counted thirty-one waiting on the platform when the train finally ground to a halt, hissing with steam and belching smoke into the frosty air.

Among the first passengers to board, Gabriel clambered up and made his way into the first car. He found a seat next to a very old man who was holding a bowler hat in his lap and had a wooden cane hooked over his arm. He nodded at Gabriel, and looked somewhat askance at his dishevelled appearance. Gabriel felt he owed the man an explanation, but realized it was too long a story so just smiled at him.

Soon they were joined by a mother and son, who sat opposite them with a great deal of fretting and fussing. The mother tried to clean the child's face by spitting on her handkerchief and reaching out to wipe him, but he squirmed and wriggled so vigorously, she eventually gave up.

To Gabriel's great relief, the train got under way and soon they were heading southwest past snow-covered farms, rivers and endless forests.

~

Around the breakfast table at the admiral's house, Chambers and Gilchrist were busy eating when Emma entered the room. She looked pale and her eyes were red from crying.

"Ah Emma, my dear," said the admiral, "there you are. There's been some news."

Emma's face brightened and she hastened to her uncle's side. "What is it? Is he alright?"

"Now, please calm yourself. Please sit down."

"Is it bad news? Please tell me, Uncle."

"I wouldn't say it was either good or bad, but I would say it is encouraging. You see, they have done a careful air search of the eastern shore and, while they have found wreckage of plane—you knew that already—they have found no sign of a body."

Emma started to sob.

"What is important, my dear, is that no body has been found. So that is cause for a certain degree of optimism."

"I suppose so," said Emma, rising.

"Won't you try to eat a little breakfast?"

"No, I couldn't manage even a mouthful. In any case, I have to get off to work."

"Emma! Surely you don't have to go in today! You're not well enough. You've had quite a shock."

"Believe me, Uncle, it's better that I go in. I'd go mad just sitting around the house."

She kissed her uncle's cheek and left. Much moved by her distress, the admiral sighed deeply.

"If she'd never met that American, none of this would have happened." Nigel Gilchrist said.

"Nigel, I don't regard a penetrating glance into the obvious as a helpful contribution," said the admiral, staring at him with distaste. "Now go and have the car brought round."

Gilchrist returned the admiral's stare, hurt and not understanding his superior's hostility.

"Now!" Chambers barked.

Gilchrist jumped like a startled rabbit and scurried out of the room.

~

Amid a horde of pedestrians, Emma and Theresa made their way along a street dirty with slush. The former was withdrawn and her face showed signs of a sleepless night.

They reached the entrance to the Richmond School, where a group of nuns cast disapproving glances at Theresa, to which she responded by smiling and tossing her flaming hair.

"Nothing is certain yet, Em. You've got to hold out hope that they'll find him."

"Thanks, T. You're a good friend," said Emma, hugging her.

"I wish I could stay with you today."

"So do I!"

"Just try to make it through the day. I'll come and get you later."

Sniffing, Emma nodded and slowly headed towards the factory.

~

In company with a dozen or more of his fellow cadets, William Chambers sauntered along the main hallway of the Naval Academy. They stopped outside the door to their classroom.

"Another boring class to look forward to. I can't wait to get to sea. What are we doing this morning, Wilcox?"

"Celestial Navigation, if you can believe it."

"God, it's going to be a dull day."

~

Francis Mackey's two boys, Douglas and Ronald, were playing in the small, frozen backyard which overlooked the harbour and narrows. They were zooming around with a model airplane, shooting imaginary Germans. Lillian watched them from the kitchen window.

Suddenly Ronald spotted *Imo* moving from Bedford Basin towards The Narrows. "Look at that! That's a big one," he said.

His brother stopped and looked at the ship. "She's moving pretty fast too. I don't think she should be going that fast."

"Dad will straighten them out, right sharpish."

"Yeah," said Doug.

~

LeMedec and Mackey, both carrying tin cups of steaming coffee, joined Glotin and Levesque on the bridge.

"*Bonjour*, Levesque," said the captain, "Full head of steam?"

"*Oui*, full head."

"We should be getting our signal from *HMS Niobe* any moment," said Mackey.

The men stood in silence, except for the slurping of coffee, staring expectantly ahead.

Suddenly, a flashing lamp aboard *Niobe* drew their attention to a rating carrying signal flags.

"Ah there it is!" LeMedec cried.

Mackey read the signal:

mont blanc hoist identification proceed bedford basin to await orders.

"You have the code from Commander Murray, Captain?"

"Of course. Levesque, run it up! Glotin, *levez l'ancre!*"

"*Oui, mon capitaine. levez l'ancre!*"

LeMedec took out some black cheroots. He offered one to Mackey, who declined, then lit one for himself. They sipped the remainder of their coffee.

"*L'ancre est bien attachée, mon capitaine,*" Glotin announced.

"Mr. Mackey, I will give you my ship."

"Thank you, captain," said Mackey, moving into position behind the helm. "Half speed ahead!"

"*En avant à demi-vitesse!*" repeated Le Medec.

"*En avant à demi-vitesse!*" Glotin shouted into the voice pipe to Legat in the engine room.

The sea churned behind the old vessel's stern and, slowly, the freighter began to move

~

At mid channel rode *HMS Highflyer*, a 5,600 ton protected cruiser. Captain Garnett and Commander Triggs stood on deck watching the first traffic of the day. Ahead they could see *Mont Blanc* moving sluggishly in their direction.

"That's a slow one, captain," observed Triggs. "She's going to have some trouble keeping up when the convoy leaves. What's that on her deck?"

"Looks like they've stacked it with drums. And did a damned sloppy job of it, too. Don't know what's in 'em."

"Hmm," Triggs grunted. "Frankly, Garnett, I'd rather not know."

Highflyer and *Mont Blanc* slowly passed. The former lowered its ensign to acknowledge their process.

~

Not far away, aboard the tug *Hilford*, Commander Murray and his helmsman, Hemings, were making their harbour patrol. They were just south of the Richmond district when Hemmings sighted *Imo* entering The Narrows on the Dartmouth side of the channel.

Murray was leaning out, scrutinizing vessels berthed on the Halifax side, when Hemmings tapped him on the shoulder. "Commander, take a look at that!"

Murray turned sharply and looked where Hemmings was pointing. "Christ Almighty!"

He whipped up his binoculars and trained them at the oncoming ship. "*Imo*. Norwegian. What the hell is she playing at? She's in the wrong water. Who's the bloody pilot?"

"Hayes, I think, William Hayes."

"I'll have his bloody job for this!" Murray said. "She's also going much too fast. She should bloody well get over into her own water right away!"

~

The men on the bridge on *Mont Blanc* had also seen *Imo* heading in their direction, and were starting to be concerned.

"*Mon Dieu!*" LeMedec cried. "Mackey, look at that ship. What is she doing?"

"Who the hell is she? Glotin, can you see?"

"*Imo*, Mr. Mackey."

"Oh right. Then Billy Hayes should be at the wheel. What the fuck is he trying to pull?"

"It look like the idiot plan to come through our water."

"Jesus Christ! She'd bloody well better not try it. Give her a blast on the whistle, Glotin. That should straighten her out."

When Glotin hesitated, LeMedec shouted at him.

"*Le sifflet, Glotin, immediatement!*"

Glotin jumped to the command, and one loud hoot echoed over the harbour.

"Just to be safe, I'm going to move over closer to the Dartmouth side," said Mackey.

Imo continued to come straight at them. As she did, she issued two blasts meaning that, contrary to all rules, they believed they had the right of way. The men on Mont Blanc could not believe their ears.

"Billy Hayes, you fucking fool!" Mackey cursed.

"*Sacre bleu!* She is moving even further into our water!"

Mont Blanc gave another hoot. Once again *Imo* responded with two hoots. Mackey and LeMedec were apoplectic with disbelief, rage and panic.

"*Idiots! Imbéciles! C'est incroyable!*"

"Maniacs! It looks as if she has no intention of correcting her course. She's taking over our water. Stop the engines immediately!"

LeMedec screamed into the voice pipe, as Glotin frantically clanged the throttle. "*Legat, arrêtez les moteurs! Arrêtez les moteurs!*"

An unstoppable juggernaut, *Imo* bore down upon them. Mackey, bathed in perspiration, exchanged rapid glances with LeMedec as both simultaneously realized there was only one option now open to them.

"Yes, by God. We must take her water, or we're done for! Start engines, and it's hard to port!"

"*Moteurs à pleine! Brutale à bâbord!*"

The engines kicked in again with a throaty rumble as Mackey furiously spun the wheel. Shaking with fear, Levesque and Glotin crossed themselves.

Imo steamed relentlessly forward as Mackey slowly, painfully veered *Mont Blanc* to her left and towards the Halifax side of the channel. They watched as she sluggishly swung to port, and heaved a sigh of relief when they saw *Imo* appear off their starboard bow. The two ships were now on parallel courses, each in the channels where the other should have been.

'Thank God," said Mackey. "I thought we were done for!"

Glotin wiped his brow with a spotted handkerchief. Le Medec sat down heavily. Levesque uttered a silent prayer of thanks to the heavens.

Jeremy Akerman

17

Just as Mackey and the *Mont Blanc* officers were silently celebrating their deliverance, the air was rent again by *Imo*'s piercing blasts. Terrifying them to the core, the sound came like three blaring trumpets in a row. Wild-eyed in utter incredulity, they stared at one another.

"*Merde!*" cursed Le Medec.

"I can't believe it," said Mackey hoarsely, "She's putting her engines full astern! Who are these lunatics?"

Mackey's and Le Medec's eyes met; they were both thinking the same thing.

"If she does that the current will swing her bow to starboard!" said the captain.

"And she will strike us!" Mackey cried.

Glotin buried his face in his hands and Levesque stood as if in a trance, while Mackey spun the wheel in a desperate effort to avoid a collision.

Le Medec stared at the other vessel as if trying to will her away, but, exactly as they had foreseen, the bow of Imo was slowly, inexorably moving towards their starboard bow.

"*O, Bon Dieu, Bon Dieu! C'est une catastrophe!*" Le Medec's voice was low and dolorous.

The *Imo*'s reversed engines failed to stop her forward drift and ponderously, relentlessly her bow inched forward. There was an ear-splitting screech of tearing metal as the *Imo* ploughed into *Mont Blanc*'s starboard side and, with a dramatic shower of sparks, cut through the steel plates of the for'ard hold.

The impact smashed Le Medec, Glotin and Levesque into the bulkhead of the wheelhouse. Only Mackey, who was hugging the wheel, was able to see what was happening out on deck.

The bow of *Imo* continued to cut through *Mont Blanc* like a knife in butter, a fountain of sparks dropping in all directions. On the deck, where the sparks were landing like rain drops, Mackey could see a light yellow liquid pouring from several of the ruptured metal drums. A sickly sweet odour and thin wisps of smoke drifted from the deck. Other drums, freed from their restraining cables, madly careened and bounced around, a few spectacularly bursting, expelling their contents high into the air.

~

From *Hilford*, Murray watched helplessly.

"What can we do, Commander?" asked Hemmings.

"Send this message immediately: Admiral Chambers Naval Command. Collision between Imo and Mont Blanc in harbour Narrows. Fire on board...."

At Naval Command, the admiral, Glichrist and several other officers crowded behind the signals officer, who read them Murray's message.

....situation utmost seriousness immediate measures required dispatch all available fire-fighting equipment urge the entire area be evacuated proceeding to shore to speak with you personally"

"Evacuate the area? Why is he talking like that?" Gilchrest asked.

"Because he knows more than you do, Nigel," said the admiral quietly.

The *Imo*'s reverse propulsion now pulled her back from the collision, and as she withdrew from the huge slash in the other ship they again harshly scraped together. The metal screamed in protest and again tall showers of sparks flew all over the decks, igniting more of the pale liquid which was still pouring from ruptured drums on *Mont Blanc*'s deck. Flames, small at first, grew rapidly and then leapt into the air. The smoke became thicker and blacker as polyaromatic hydrocarbons were released.

Fire on *Mont Blanc* spread rapidly, engulfing the entire foredeck. Flaming rivers of benzene surged through the rends in the steel plates of Number One Hold.

A seaman staggered, screaming, onto the deck, his clothes flaming around him until he leapt into the sea. Other crew members appeared, running about in panic. Dense black smoke was now billowing from *Mont Blanc*, making visibility almost impossible.

Frozen with shock, Le Medec watched the flames leap over the foredeck. Thick clouds rolled over the windows of the bridge.

Mackey's face hardened with the belief that the only correct course of action was clear. "Captain Le Medec. Listen to me. We must bring her about!"

"*Non! C'est impossible.*" The captain shook his head. "No. *Jetez l'ancre*! Drop anchor. Those are my orders."

"No, we must try to get her out to sea. If we can flood the hold maybe we can put out the fire. We must get water into the hold!"

"*Non, non!*"

"We should try to get the ship away from the harbour if we can. We have a responsibility to all the people who live and work here. Don't you see that?"

"Jettez L'ancre!" Le Medec said stubbornly. "Levesque, *Obéis à mes orders!"*

"For God's sake, bring her about!"

Nobody made a move. They stared at each other as flames started licking at the bridge widows.

At that moment, Legat, his face covered in soot, burst in. "That stuff is everywhere. Pouring below decks. The engine room is on fire. Captain, what are we going to do?'

Le Medec hesitated for a split second, then turned deliberately to Mackey. "We will abandon ship. *Abandonnez le navire!"*

"If we abandon her, she could drift towards shore, where thousands of people live and work," Mackey pleaded. "We should at least try to get her as far up the harbour as possible."

"I am the captain of this ship, Mr. Mackey. My word is the law. We will abandon ship. Glotin, Levesque, Legat, *abandonner le navire maintenant!"*

The other officers immediately raced off the bridge. Seven short blasts followed by one long blast were sounded on the ship's whistle. Again and again it rang through the crippled ship.

"You should think of your cargo, Captain," said Mackey sternly.

"I am thinking of my cargo, Mr. Mackey!" Le Medec responded, and walked out.

Knowing he was beaten, Mackey followed him.

~

At Naval Command, Admiral Chambers and his staff watched in silence as they saw flames now engulfing *Mont Blanc*.

The admiral turned to his signals officer. "Signal *Highflyer*. To Captain Garnet: All available equipment to *Mont Blanc* to get fire under control."

~

Mont Blanc's port lifeboat, hanging amidships, was released and splashed into the water. Seconds later the starboard boat was also released. Ropes and ladders were quickly thrown down and crew members poured down in a frenzy. Above their heads another barrel of benzene exploded, sending a fireball high into the sky.

~

On *Highflyer*, Garnett, Triggs, Lieutenant Ruffles, and the signals officer received the admiral's message with disbelief.

"It all very well to tell us to send everything we

have, but what do we have, Commander?" Garnett asked.

"Most of our vessels are gone. The steam cutter and sailing pinnace are in Dartmouth, landing stokers. We could send the whaler, I suppose."

"Will you head up that party, please? There's no time to waste.'

"Certainly. I'll take Ruffles with me."

~

The starboard lifeboat was now almost full as Le Medec, Glotin and Levesque joined the company. The boat moved off toward the Dartmouth shore.

Still on board Mackey found Legat waiting to board the port lifeboat. "Legat, tell me honestly, could we restart the engines?"

"*Oui*, Monsieur, but it would take fifteen minutes to get any propulsion. I don't think we have that kind of time."

At that moment, another drum of benzene exploded.

"No, you're right," Mackey agreed ruefully. He took one last look at the ship, then followed Legat down the ladder into the lifeboat.

Mont Blanc, its front half completely consumed by flames, now twisted in the current and started to drift towards the Halifax shore.

~

An apprehensive Murray fretted in the *Hillford* wheelhouse. Hemmings was gunning the engine in an attempt to get to the docks.

"Damn! She's drifting fast towards the Halifax piers. That's all we need. For God's sake go faster."

"I'm doing my best, Commander. We're already going flat out."

~

Emma was sitting despondently at her desk, reviewing the weekly payroll, when a knock on her door announced an embarrassed seamstress. Another female worker was looking over her shoulder.

"Excuse me, Miss Emma. Have you heard? There's a ship on fire in the harbour."

"No, I hadn't heard," said Emma, going to the window. She could just see *Mont Blanc* in the distance.

"We were wondering—"

"—if you could watch from my office. Yes, of course, provided it is alright with your supervisor."

"Thank you Miss. Yes, we cleared it with Mrs Jennings. She's right behind us."

~

Both lifeboats were now well on their way to the Dartmouth shore, the starboard boat some way ahead of the port boat. As they progressed and the *Mont Blanc* drifted, the distance between them widened. In his boat, Le Medec sat motionless, his head in his hands. In the other boat, Mackey surveyed the scene behind him with increasing consternation

~

At Naval Command, the admiral and his staff nervously watched the fiery *Mont Blanc* drift towards the dock. Chambers and Gilchrist had been joined by Petty Officer Carter and Pitcairn, the duty officer.

"She's coming on fast," said the admiral, "At that speed she'll hit the wharf with a hell of a force. Carter, get down there and make sure the wharf is clear of all personnel."

"Aye, aye, sir!"

"Nigel, take the car. Drive him down."

"Yes, admiral."

The young officer dashed out of the office and clattered along the corridor and down the stairs.

Less quickly, Gilchrist followed.

~

Douglas and Ronald Mackey would have been late for school if they did not hurry, but they saw a group of people at the crest of a hill, and wandered over to see what was going on.

A boy of Ronald's age cried out to them. "Ronnie, Dougie, c'mere! There's a ship afire."

They rushed over and saw the flaming *Mont Blanc* and the listless *Imo*.

"That's the big one we seen before," said Douglas.

"Yeah, it is. Where's Dad at, I wonder. Is he out there?"

"I don't think he coulda been. He would never allow this."

~

Mont Blanc bore down upon the dock, and when she was seconds away from impact, Petty Officer Carter ran out onto the planking to see if anyone was still in the way of danger.

He had only time to shout out that the area should be evacuated when the blazing ship ploughed into and through the wharf with a loud crunching sound, snapping the huge timbers like matchsticks and hurling them into the air. Carter took a large chunk of piling directly in the face and was killed instantly.

The ship cut completely into the dock, coming to a halt only after smashing into one of the buildings. Immediately, the broken timber of the building caught fire.

Gilchrist, who had been protected by the admiral's car, restarted the engine and headed back to Naval Command as fast as he could.

~

When he returned, Gilchrist found the place in turmoil. That the tension was rising was palpable.

"Pitcairn, get on to the city fire department. Tell them they'll have to send all the equipment they can lay their hands on."

"At once, admiral!"

The admiral stood at the window, impatiently tapping his fingers on the ledge.

Pitcairn returned. "They said they'll do their best, sir."

"Hmm. I hope their best will be good enough."

"Admiral?"

"Yes, Pitcairn?"

"If I might ask a question, sir?"

"Yes, what is it?"

"In Commander Murray's message, he spoke of evacuating the whole area. Did he mean just the dock or—?"

"The whole area?"

"Yes, I did wonder. Which did he mean?'

"I'm sorry to say, Pitcairn, that the Commander meant everything. The whole shebang, as the Americans say."

"Why, sir?"

"Because *Mont Blanc* is loaded to the gunwales with tons and tons of high explosives."

"Does that mean—?"

"We may soon find out, Pitcairn, although we might not live to tell the tale."

"Will you tell anybody else, sir?"

"Murray knows. Also the pilot, Mackey. But there doesn't seem much point in telling anyone else. It is not as if it could help them get out of danger in time. Don't you agree?"

"I suppose I do," Pitcairn said, swallowing hard. "And, sir, how much time might that be?"

"We might have a quarter of an hour. It's just a guess. It could be only minutes. Are you alright, Pitcairn?"

"Excuse me sir. I think I have to go to the lavatory."

The young officer rushed from the room.

~

On *Hilford*, Hemmings and Murray saw *Highflyer*'s whaler coming towards them.

"Looks like help is on the way, sir."

"Good."

"And over there too."

"It's *Stella Maris*. Well this may make a difference."

Commanded by Captain Horatio Brannen, the steam tug *Stella Maris* reached *Mont Blanc* and immediately her crew commenced to try to get the fire under control with the stream of a single hose. The ship's hull was now so hot that clouds of steam rose as the water met it.

Around about, several wharves and warehouses were now in flames and billows of black smoke blocked out the sky.

Commander Triggs stood in the whaler's bow as it sliced through the water at top speed. He yelled to his helmsman to bring her alongside *Stella Maris*. He grabbed a line from the tug and hauled himself aboard.

It was blisteringly hot on deck and the crew in their winter clothing were profusely sweating as they moved urgently about their tasks.

"Where's your captain?" Triggs asked a rating, and was directed to where Captain Brannen was supervising the men with the hose.

"Captain, Commander Triggs of *HMS Highflyer* at your service. Is this the only hose we have?"

"Yes, 'fraid so," said Brannen "Little good it's doing. We'd have better luck trying to piss on it."

"Then, do you agree with me that we should try to tow *Mont Blanc* away from shore. We might save some shore buildings and have a better chance with the fire if we're in open water."

"Agreed, Triggs. Between us, we may be able to do that."

Triggs walked back to the rail and called to Ruffles on the whaler. "Ruffles, what kind of line do we have?"

"Five inch only, sir."

"Damn! Well it'll have to do. Bring it out and take it up."

Ruffles and a rating from Trigg's crew climbed up one of the ladders left dangling from *Mont Blanc* when it was abandoned by its crew. With much difficulty, they carried the heavy line, and when their feet touched the hull, the soles of their boots smoked against the hot metal.

Ruffles and the rating secured the line aboard the crippled freighter while Triggs and Brannen did likewise on *Stella Maris*. All four men were coughing violently from the intense heat and thick smoke.

They watched the towing line tighten as the tug backed slowly into the channel. But the line started to fray, then loudly snapped, its end whipping down not far from them.

"Damnation!" Triggs cursed.

"I have another," said Brannen. "We'll try that."

~

As the lifeboats from *Mont Blanc* came close to the Dartmouth shoreline, Mackey and some of the French ratings jumped out and in deep water pulled the boats to ground. When they scraped over the shingle, the remainder of the crew got out.

Immediately, Mackey took charge, pointing inland. "We must head for the woods. It's our only hope if she blows."

Le Medec, who seemed to have snapped out of his funk, nodded furiously in agreement and urged his men onward. "Vers les bois! Au forêt!" he shouted.

They scrambled over boulders, up a bank and down the other side into scrubland. The woods were a hundred tantalizing yards away.

~

Meanwhile, Gabriel's train had been speeding

through the Nova Scotia countryside, and was now in the outer suburbs of Halifax. The fussy woman and her son had both been asleep since they passed Fall River. He tried to strike up a conversation with the old man, but all he could get were monosyllabic responses. He was very tired, extremely hungry and felt excessively filthy.

He rejoiced when he heard the conductor tell another passenger that they would shortly be at their destination.

~

Commander Murray and his men had been running along the entire waterfront, trying to alert any remaining people to the potential danger. He reached the dockside telegraph office and rushed in.

Seated inside were Vincent Coleman and William Lovett, regular employees of the Telegraph company. They were startled by Murray's sudden entrance and even more by his message.

"Everybody out! Run like hell! *Mont Blanc* is on fire and she could blow at any minute!"

The men hesitated, looking at each other.

"Out you fools! Now!"

Murray dashed away and the men ran after him, but Coleman suddenly turned back.

"What the hell are you doing?" Demanded Lovett. "You heard what the man said."

"I know, but what about the trains that are coming in? They should be warned."

"There's no time, Vince! You do what you like. I'm getting the hell out of here!"

Lovett ran off towards the city, as Coleman turned and walked back to the office. He sat down, pulled his Morse key towards him and started to tap.

Having finished sending, he breathed a sigh of relief and rose from his desk. The clock on the wall showed 9.06 am.

~

From *Stella Maris*, Brannen and Triggs anxiously watched as Ruffles tried to secure another tow line to *Mont Blanc*. They were exhausted and suffering from smoke inhalation, but pressed on with their task.

~

The train was just entering the Rockingham district when, with a deafening screech, the brakes slammed on. Some passengers who were standing were sent flying down the aisles. Overhead baggage came crashing to the floor, one of the woman's packages hitting Gabriel on the shoulder. The woman screamed and the child began to howl.

The old man clutched his bowler hat. "Why have we stopped?" he asked in a thin, reedy voice.

"I don't know, sir," said Gabriel.

18

With an ear-splitting, staccato roar and a blinding white flash, *Mont Blanc* and everything in its vicinity disintegrated in a gigantic, searing ball of flaming gasses. With the exception of the masts, the super-structure of the 5,000 ton *Imo* disappeared from its deck level, and its hull, still bearing the words 'Belgian Relief', was lifted bodily out of the water and flung through the air 200 yards across the channel onto the shingle of the Dartmouth shore. The impact was inaudible because the shock waves of the explosion rendered all human and animal hearing disabled.

Half-way out of the door of the telegraph office, Vincent Coleman was melted into nothingness as the building was blasted into oblivion.

Along the dockside, every pier, wharf, and jetty erupted and, twisted and disintegrating, was hurled into the sky. The sea boiled like a giant cauldron, totally swamping all smaller boats.

The roar continued in a deadening, pulsating pattern as an enormous crack appeared in the bed of the harbour, rapidly increasing in length and width. Those fish which had not been killed by heat or benzene poisoning darted about in panic. Then millions of gallons of water poured into the chasm, sucking all fish and detritus of the sea bed with it.

As the harbour's water was drawn into the submarine canyon, the sea level dramatically dropped by several feet as if the areas were being drained by a huge sink.

The three large windows in Admiral Chamber's office imploded with ferocious velocity. Gilchrist, Pitcairn and the signal officer were hurled against the rear wall and were impaled to it by long slivers of broken glass. Chambers was thrown from his desk to the door, smashing it down in the process, and was showered with bricks from a collapsing wall.

In the dockland area to the south of the explosion site, the giant cranes and derricks buckled, broke and were sent whirling into a sky already filled with flying debris of every description. The pulsating, unheard roar continued unabated.

Lillian Mackey was scrubbing the kitchen floor when the bursting window showered her with glass, the roof and upper floor disappeared, and the entire wall crashed down, trapping her underneath.

Huge cracks appeared in the ground surface all

over the city, spreading uphill and downhill from street to street, from district to district. In the path of these ever-extending fissures gas pipes, previously buried beneath the streets, now heaved, twisted and burst. Gas rushed into the air and, in many places, ignited. Roaring plumes of flame leapt high into the air.

A large brick building, the Acadia Sugar Refinery, was instantly demolished by the blast, its tall chimney stack crumbling like cheese. Employees who had gathered on the refinery roof to watch *Mont Blanc* on fire were killed instantly and were spouted into the sky like toy soldiers.

Theresa and her pupils had just started their lesson when the classroom was flooded with a brilliant white light. The overwhelming thrust of the blast swept through the school, imploding all windows and hurling deadly shards of glass into the children's faces.

The immense throbbing of the shock wave hit the train station, demolishing it at a stroke, and just beyond, in the rail yard, a large iron bridge was ripped from its foundations and catapulted upwards. The rails themselves rose up like hundreds of giant snakes writhing in the air.

At the Naval Academy the shock waves punched through the windows of the main classroom, spitting a fusillade of glass splinters. Most of the wall followed as if sucked by an enormous Hoover, and the cadets were showered with broken glass, plaster and masonry.

William, at the back of the room, threw himself to the floor behind his desk, thus avoiding worse injury, but his face, neck and upper arms were studded with glass shards and he was bleeding profusely.

Murray was striding up one of the few docks not demolished, shouting warnings left and right, when the ground opened in front of him. He swerved to avoid the gaping fissure but, as he did, was struck and killed by flying timbers.

~

The sucking of the harbour water into the sea bed chasm, and the consequent lowering of the water level, created a build-up of pressure to fill the void, and a sixteen-foot tidal wave, which had been forming in the outer reaches of the harbour, now moved inexorably towards the inner harbour. In Bedford Basin, littered with debilitated and capsized ships swirling about like leaves in a rain barrel, another tidal wave built and moved towards The Narrows.

In parts of the city, every wooden building was instantaneously razed to the ground, and the spires of three churches were flung into the streets. Just audible above the pulsating roar came the crazed, incongruous ringing of church bells as their towers crumbled to the ground, and the bells rolled around in the streets.

At the admiral's house, Mrs. Chambers was sitting in the dining room window taking breakfast, waited upon by Cameron, the butler. Since the room faced west, first a deafening, sickening crack came from the direction of the harbour, then the room's east wall bulged like a giant bowl before bursting inwards, inundating its occupants with laths, plaster, and splintered woodwork. Then the windows blew outwards, sucking Mrs. Chambers and Cameron from the room and hurling them into the snow-covered garden beyond.

In the Dominion Textile Factory, Emma was kneeling, putting documents into the heavy safe which sat on the floor between herself and the window. She heard the blast, then her hearing vanished and she was exposed to a vicious barrage of glass and debris. Terrified, she crouched behind the safe, screaming with fear.

On the second floor, a huge crack appeared along the floor's centre line and the two concrete halves swung downwards. The big, heavy looms and other machinery snapped away from their footings and, together with furniture and workers, plunged into the chasm. Soon, the roof collapsed and also fell inwards.

In a square in front of a large, three-story warehouse was a rambling, open-air market, its stalls selling everything from fish to hardware and dry goods. Suddenly, the square was bathed in brilliant light, then the blast pounded through, hitting the warehouse and tearing everything in the market to shreds. Those who survived grabbed their ears in agony and huddled onto a heaving ground surface. Those still able to see apprehended that the warehouse had ceased to exist.

The sky rained pots, pans, tools, canvas, timbers, masonry, severed limbs, dead pigs, sides of beef, and dozens of—amazingly—still-fluttering, squawking chickens.

The huge tidal wave, a giant wall of water coming in from the ocean, gained momentum and thundered towards George's Island, swamping and sweeping over everything in its wake. The larger ships, which survived with only their superstructures damaged by the initial blast, now were buffeted and tossed towards the shore, some being capsized in the process.

The ocean's tidal wave's northern counterpart now started to roll like a juggernaut out of Bedford Basin and into The Narrows.

The sky over the entire area darkened as the gigantic pall of black smoke spread and settled. Among the billowing clouds and fumes, huge rocks from the sea bed, funnels and masts of ships, timbers from wharves, twisted iron from bridges, cranes and grotesque body parts of dead victims were swirled and tossed by the force of the blast. Several streets in the area north-west of the harbour were bathed in a blinding white light, and row after row of poorer wooden houses and tenements were instantly flattened and reduced to rubble.

The tidal waves, now of increasingly dramatic proportions, swept into the central area from north and south and met with a thunderous ferocity, swamping boats and engulfing the shorelines on both sides. The now combined force of these waves swept over the docks and surged up into the steep streets of the lower town. Great walls of water rolled over flattened buildings and, swirling timbers and masonry in their wake, advanced and destroyed.

The fleeing crew of *Mont Blanc* were running through the trees when the greenness turned to whiteness and the sound of crows was overwhelmed by the roar. Most of the surrounding trees had their top two-thirds blown off, while others were twisted and wrenched from their roots. Broken branches and twigs in their thousands flew about them, and

Mackey was tossed into the lower branches of a still-standing spruce.

Glotin, Levesque and Legat had parts of their clothing ripped off as they were flung headlong into the snow.

The water which had pushed up into the city streets, now receded rapidly and poured back into the harbour. As it returned it built up in the channel, creating two new waves which swept towards the sea in one direction and into Bedford Basin in the other. Boats which had previously been assaulted were buffeted and swamped for a second time. Smaller vessels disappeared under the waves, while larger ships were rolled on their sides, where they shipped hundreds of gallons of water.

Gabriel, the train conductor, and some passengers were standing around by the side of the tracks, and other travellers were hanging out of the windows, when they heard the blast and saw the sky fill with dazzling, incandescent light. Then a monstrous wind tore along the tracks, loudly rattling the train and knocking people to the ground.

Far out at sea, a merchant vessel was contemplating its approach to Halifax when the men on the bridge heard the blast and saw the ghastly light. Suddenly, off the port bow they saw a massive wall of water, fifteen feet high, rolling towards them. The captain and mate watched incredulously as the huge wave relentlessly bore down on the ship.

"What the hell is that?" the mate asked.

"There must have been an earthquake," said the captain. "Turn into it immediately and go with it. It's our only chance not to be overturned!"

The mate desperately swung the wheel so the wave would not take them amidships. The captain stared, mesmerized by what he was watching. He had been at sea, man and boy, for forty years but had never witnessed anything like this.

Eighty-five miles away, in Harrigan's Cove, the Wambolts' windows and doors shook violently and cups and saucers fell to the floor broken. Harold said he heard "the most God awful noise" which sent his fowl squawking in all directions, and drove the dog to cower under the stairs. Margaret said she did not know what was going on, but she knew it was something of a heavenly nature which might bring Gabriel back to her.

Some miles closer to Halifax, an old farmhouse sat in a grassy dell looking due west onto rolling, but snowy fields. The farmer and his son stood in the yard watching the black cloud which was blotting out the sun. A strange noise, like the rumbling of empty drums, suddenly filled the air and a great wind rushed around them. Another noise, almost a whine, suffused them and, looking up, to their amazement they saw an enormous lump of twisted ship's hull whistling past them. This huge projectile smashed into the barn, totally demolishing the structure and scattering its beams and timbers like matchwood.

The farmer and his son looked at each other in a state of stupefaction.

"My heavens, Randy, what was that?"

"'Twas the wrath of God, father," replied his son.

19

With some difficulty, Legat helped Mackey out of the tree in which he had become entangled. When he managed to clamber down, he was cut and bleeding. So were most of the officers and crew of *Mont Blanc* who were extricating themselves from underbrush and unearthed tree roots.

Movement was nearly impossible due to the thousands of broken branches and the overturned trunks of trees. Picking a painful path through the destruction, Mackey made his way towards Le Medec and Glotin, the latter of whom was streaming with blood from his head.

"You okay, Glotin?"

"As far as I know. I think it is coming from my scalp."

"How about you, Captain?"

"*Pas mal*, Mr. Mackey. Something has happened to my leg—I don't know what—and these cuts on my face."

Mackey looked around at the rest of the company.

Some were standing, clutching tree stumps, some were sitting, nursing their wounds, and some were lying motionless. "It looks like some of our friends were not as lucky as we were," said Mackey, "If I was you, Captain, I would call the roll."

"*Quoi*?"

"Call the names of your crew to find out who is here and who may be missing."

"*Ah oui*. Glotin, would you do that, please?"

From their various locations in the woods, the officers and crew responded as Glotin called out their names.

"Levesque?"

"*Içi.*"

"Legat?"

"*Içi.*"

"Beauchamps?"

"*Içi.*"

"Thomas?"

"*Içi.*"

"Brun?"

This continued until all forty crew members were accounted for. Each was found to be in reasonable shape, given the circumstances, except for young Quenier, who was badly injured and could not move without assistance.

"Everyone survived!" Le Medec said with obvious

satisfaction. *"C'est un miracle!"*

"It certainly is," said Mackey. "I wonder how many of those crazy bastards on *Imo* escaped."

~

The blast and the tsunami that followed had thrown *Imo* ashore on the Dartmouth side of Halifax Harbour. When the smoke cleared and the ship, heavily listing to starboard, had settled into the shallows, it was not possible for Captain Haakon From to take a roll call because he was dead. So were First Officer Albert Iverson and four other crew members.

So was pilot Billy Hayes. If ever he had an explanation to offer for what had occurred, the world would never hear it.

~

Passengers congregated in groups along the railway tracks, watching the enormous black cloud mushrooming in the near distance. Clearly, all was in disarray and nobody knew what to do, so Gabriel strode along the line to a signal box and accosted the man who had just descended.

"What happened? Do you know?"

"Yeah. I got this telegram just before the blast," the

man replied, passing it to Gabriel.

> stop train immediately stop munitions ship on fire in harbour goodbye

"If the train had kept going,", the signalman said, "it would likely have been blown to pieces."

"My God! How long before it will be able to move?"

"I don't know, sir. I'd only be guessing, but if it is as bad up ahead as I think it is, it could be days or weeks before she can move."

"I can't wait," Gabriel said. "I must get into the city!"

"Everyone else will be trying to get out of the city. Why in hell do you want to get in?'

"My fiancée is there. I must find her."

"I wish you luck," said the signalman, "but I wouldn't fancy your chances."

"How far is it into Halifax? I'm an American. I don't know this area."

"I figure it's about ten miles. That would be on a clear road, but I doubt you're going to find anything ahead which is not in an uproar. Likely the roads will be blocked."

~

Admiral Chambers groaned as he slowly regained consciousness. Piece by piece, he pushed off the bricks, woodwork and plaster which covered him, and then, after several attempts, heaved away the desk which had collapsed on him. He had a large, ugly gash on his forehead and cuts across his nose, chin and neck.

When he looked up it was into an empty sky. It was snowing. In addition to the roof, the entire east wall had disappeared.

Unsteadily, he hauled himself up and staggered about, trying to get his bearings. A door was hanging weirdly from half a frame. In disgust, the admiral kicked it down with a single blow. It crashed, sending up clouds of dust.

Everywhere was wreckage. Wood, masonry, bricks, plaster, compasses, binoculars, mortar, books, charts, furniture were scattered this way and that.

What caught his gaze, and kept it, was the grotesque sight of Pitcairn, Nigel Gilchrist, and the signal officer, all obviously dead, impaled to the wooden panelling of the west wall by long, deadly, shards of glass from the blasted windows. Snow sat on the heads and shoulders of the three dead officers.

~

Mackey and Le Medec stood, watching Levesque and Glotin attending to the wounds of the injured crew members. The snow was now coming down heavily.

"I have to thank you, M. Mackey, for all your assistance, despite our earlier disagreement. I do not think the outcome would have been different whatever we did."

"It is hard to say. Maybe you're right. So, no hard feelings."

"*Quoi?*"

"I don't know how to say it in your language."

"*Pas d'émotions fortes*," suggested Legat, who was nearby, propped up by a tree trunk.

"*Ah! Mais non!* Not at all."

The three men exchanged handshakes. Glotin and Levesque came forward and did likewise.

"Well, you're on your own now. I have to get back to the other side. I have to report and then find my family—if they are still alive."

"*Courage, mon ami*," said Le Medec, "*Bonne chance. Que le bon Dieu soit avec vous!*"

With a brisk wave, Mackey turned back and set off in the direction of the shore.

The Frenchmen waved back. "Adieu!" they shouted.

~

Sweat pouring from his face, Gabriel stopped for breath. The train was now far behind him. It was difficult to see the great, dark cloud now because the snow was becoming thicker.

Suddenly, with a loud clattering, a beautiful black stallion raced down the track towards him, its eyes wide with fear, its saddle twisting and the reins swinging wildly.

Gabriel readied himself as the stallion approached and, as it passed him, he grabbed the reins. Jerked off his feet, he was dragged along the rails behind the powerful beast.

Feet scrambling, he managed to pull himself, hand over hand, upwards until he was able to grab the saddle and got one foot into a stirrup. The beast reared, almost throwing him to the ground, but he managed to avoid being unhorsed, and rubbing the animal's neck and making soothing sounds, eventually got it under control.

Gently, he turned the horse around and was soon galloping towards the city.

~

Eagerly, Mackey clambered over the rocks to the beach, hoping to find one of *Mont Blanc*'s lifeboats in seaworthy condition. These hopes were quickly dashed when he reached the water's edge and saw only deep depressions in the shingle. Looking seaward, he saw one boat badly smashed and sinking, and the other adrift in the channel.

Cursing, he stomped off up the beach, desperately searching for something which could take him to the other side.

What only hours ago had been a thriving boatyard was now a scene of utter devastation and confusion. Buildings had been flattened, wharves and jetties had been torn up and flung inland, and all manner of debris and detritus lay in twisted heaps.

Mackey stumbled into the yard, looking this way and that, until he found what appeared to be three suitable boats lodged among the rubble; but when he touched the first, it disintegrated. The other two had large holes in their sides.

Not far away, Mackey noticed a number of oil drums. He clattered over the debris to get to them. Examining them, he found them to be empty—which was important for buoyancy—and without holes.

He pulled them up so the tide could not carry them away, then went looking for ropes or cables. Eventually, he found various lengths of rope and cable and dragged them back to the drums. Then he hunted around until he discovered some planks which were still undamaged by the explosion and not too big or unwieldy. These, too, he dragged back to where the drums and ropes were waiting.

He found the cables were far too stiff to be of use, but with the lengths of rope he managed to lash four drums to two of the best planks.

Exhausted, but satisfied with his work, he gently pulled the contraption into the water. It floated and appeared to be relatively stable, so sitting precariously across the planks he used a third, smaller one, to paddle himself out into the channel.

Slowly, deliberately, Mackey paddled his bizarre craft across the harbour. It was difficult to maneuver and sometimes spun around in circles, but after a while he got the hang of it and started to make progress.

He was fascinated but horrified by what he saw on his journey. Everywhere were boats and ships in various states of disability. Some, having sunk, loomed in ghostly fashion just below the surface, and others had only their masts, chimneys or sterns sticking out of the water. Still others were waterlogged and eerily floated half in, half out of the water. These were highly dangerous and Mackey struggled to avoid them, as one blow from these phantoms could seriously injure if not kill him.

Some vessels were floating shells, their superstructures obliterated, others were blackened and charred hulks, infernos still belching black smoke.

The air was thick with smoke and the water was clogged with all manner of flotsam and jetsam. The visibility, not good to begin with because of all the smoke, now worsened as the snow intensified.

Every few yards, the raft bumped into human bodies, some of them grotesquely mutilated by the blast or by fire. One corpse got caught on the corner of the raft and Mackey knelt down to disengage it.

As he pushed it away, it rolled, revealing it had no arms but a revoltingly disfigured face. He recoiled in horror, vomited and lost his balance, and fell into the water. Spluttering, he frantically grabbed the edge of the planks and scrambled back on board.

As he gasped for breath, he saw that the smaller plank he had been using as a paddle had fallen overboard. Exhausted almost beyond endurance and utterly sick at heart, Mackey lay down on the raft, the water lapping over the sides, and using his arms tried to propel the makeshift vessel to shore.

He could now just see the Halifax side, but he knew it was still at least another hour before he attained his goal.

More bodies floated past, some bloated, some bright pink from breathing carbon monoxide, others hideously mutilated by projectiles of wood, steel, glass. He recognized one of the bodies as a man he had worked with in the dockyard. Strangely, he looked completely at peace.

Then, suddenly, the water was full of rubber tubing, which brought the raft to a standstill, and it took Mackey a full twenty, frustrating minutes to clear his path of this slippery obstruction.

When he was a tantalizing twenty feet from land, the current suddenly grew so strong it threatened to take him back out into the channel and down the harbour towards the sea.

In despair, he cast about for something he could latch on to and saw a semi-submerged hawser. It was immensely heavy, so he could barely hold it, but it was sufficient to swing the raft into shore.

Finally, at long last, Mackey was able to scramble onto dry land. Very shaky from his wounds and strenuous exertions, he tottered off through the twisted pilings and general wreckage towards the city. He had just undergone a sea journey he never wished to repeat.

20

Surrounded by collapsed masonry and rubble of the devastated school, Ronnie Mackey picked his way through the bodies of children. He was cut and badly bruised in many places, but was steady on his feet.

After burrowing around in the wreckage for half an hour, Ronnie finally recognized Dougie lying under several beams. The little boy was very badly cut about the face and hands and he was missing an ear where his head was a mass of congealed blood.

"Dougie! Holy Jesus! Are you alright?" Ronnie knelt down by his injured brother. "Come on, Dougie, wake up! Wake up!"

Dougie slowly stirred and opened one eye; the other was closed by a blood-hardened gash.

Ronnie tugged at the timbers and managed to create a space through which he could extricate Dougie. "Attaboy! Come on, Dougie, wake up. We got to go and find Theresa."

~

Covered with dust and pieces of rubble, Emma lay dazed on the floor behind the large safe. The roof had gone and the exterior walls had all but disappeared. Only the interior wall and its door remained intact. The air was thick with plaster dust and smoke from a nearby fire.

Emma came to her senses slowly, sat up and surveyed the despoliation around her. Only a few yards away from her were the motionless bodies of the two seamstresses who had come to her office to watch the burning of *Mont Blanc*. Crawling over, she placed her hand on one of the girl's faces and stroked her hair. There was no response, so she gave the girl a shake.

Realizing that she was dead, Emma moved to the other girl and, seeing that her head was grotesquely twisted from her neck, knew she was also past all hope. She dragged herself to her feet, stumbled to the door and pushed it open.

A fire was blazing out of control at the far end of the room and the smoke made Emma cough violently. She could hear cries of wounded people somewhere, but she was not sure where they were. So she limped towards the stairs, but slipped and fell. She struggled to get up, but fell yet again on the slippery, sticky surface of the floor.

Her hand was covered in blood and, looking

down, she saw that the floor was likewise smeared with the darkening red substance.

She screamed and rushed to the stairwell. She desperately scrambled down the stairs, stopping only at the last moment, when she saw that the entire floor of the second story had disappeared. She grabbed for the rail as her feet slipped away from under her.

"Oh God, please…"

Hanging there, she looked down and saw the first floor, heaped with looms, other machinery and concrete slabs. All around voices cried out for assistance.

Slowly, gradually, she hauled herself up and got her feet back on semi-solid masonry. She could see that the only way down to the ground was by way of a similar staircase at the other end of the room, but that to get there she would have to edge her way along a very narrow, jagged ledge which constituted the only remains of the floor.

Her legs shaking wildly, she inched her way along the ledge, chunks of which broke off under her weight and fell crashing to the lower floor. At one point, her foot slipped and, had she not found a jutting beam to cling to, she would have fallen to an almost certain death.

She hung in the air for a split second until she was

able to swing her foot on to a solid piece of the ledge. She regained her balance and resumed her tortuous journey around the room.

When she finally got down, the first floor looked like a battlefield. Blood was splashed over the remaining walls and lay about an eighth of an inch thick on the floor. Broken, twisted, cracked heavy machinery was everywhere, pinning bodies beneath it.

She could see that most of those trapped by the looms were dead, but from here and there she could hear people shrieking with pain, groaning or gurgling through their own blood. It was as much as she could do to stop herself from passing out.

As she was struggling towards the exit, a voice called out to her, "Miss Chambers! Miss Chambers! Help me. I'm over here!"

She stopped, turned and peered back through the smoke and dust. Seeing nothing, she pressed on.

"Miss Chambers! Over here, Miss Chambers!"

Looking back again, she saw through the smoke the manager, her boss, Mr. Wright, dragging himself across the floor. One of his legs was badly broken, with splintered bones outlandishly sticking through the fabric of his trousers.

Emma rushed to his side and, grabbing him by his wrists, pulled him towards the outside. As she did, his body rode over pieces of detritus and he howled with pain.

Suddenly, Emma heard a mighty crack above her head and, looking up saw a colossal piece of concrete falling from the upper building. Instinctively, she released his wrists and fell backwards, rolling away as best she could.

With a thunderous noise, the concrete came crashing straight down on top of Mr. Wright, crushing him from the chest to his feet. His widened eyes looked at her appealingly as frothy blood gurgled from his mouth.

Screaming, Emma ran from the factory and stumbled into what was once a city street.

Outside she stopped and gaped at the scene before her. Almost the entire neighbourhood had been levelled, only the occasional building still showing a wall or a chimney above the wreckage. Bodies were strewn everywhere and black smoke hung over the desolate landscape.

A young sailor came out of nowhere and placed a hand on her shoulder. Startled, she whirled around and stared at him, frozen with shock. His hair was a wild mass of tangled blood and the bottom half of his jaw had been blown away.

Screaming in panic, she tried to pull away, but his grip was strong and her dress tore as she backed off, her brooch falling to the ground with a tinkle.

Terrified, she ran madly down the street, weaving this way and that to avoid holes and obstacles.

Exhausted, Emma finally stopped running and collapsed on a heap of debris. She buried her face in her hands and started to weep uncontrollably. The snow fell steadily around her.

After a while she became so cold she decided she had to keep moving. Pulling her tattered clothing around her, she limped in what she thought, hoped, might be the direction of the Naval Academy.

When her foot got caught in something on the ground, she looked down and saw a heavy, black winter coat. Rejoicing in her good luck, she reached out and pulled it, but underneath was the lifeless, frozen body of an old priest.

Tears streaming down her cheeks she looked up into the snow-filled sky. "Oh, God, what is happening here?" she wailed.

She put on the priest's coat, buttoned it up and pulled up the collar. "May God forgive me," she said.

A little further on, Emma turned a corner into yet another devastated street. There was destruction and chaos everywhere, and the never-ending snow.

From somewhere up ahead she heard cries of "Thief! Thief! Thief!"

She staggered along towards the noise to find a

very large shopkeeper thrashing a young man with a broom. The man clutched a box of chocolates, apparently taken from what little remained of the tiny, ruined shop's supplies.

"Get away from me, you old bag!"

The shopkeeper continued to rain punishing blows to the man's head. Emma watched in disbelief.

"I'll give you, old bag, you thieving bastard!" the woman shrieked, wielding the broom even more vigorously.

Howling with pain the man wriggled away and ran off.

The woman turned on Emma, raising her broom. "What do we have here? Another thief?"

"No, indeed, ma'am," said Emma meekly.

"Good! If them Germans want my shop they'll have to deal with me first!"

"The Germans?"

"Sure, darlin'. Who else d'you think done all this?"

"How could they do that?"

"They dropped bombs from them Zeppelins. I heard tell they landed at Chebucto Head. I don't imagine it'll be long afore they gets here."

"My goodness!"

"You better get going', girl," said the woman "by all accounts, them Germans wouldn't think nothing of raping a li'l thing like you!"

"Oh my God!" Emma exclaimed.

~

In Ottawa, the Minister of Militia and National Defence, Sidney Mewburn had just arrived at his office on Sparks Street. He barely had a chance to remove and hang up his topcoat before Eugene Fiset, the Deputy Minister, rushed in a state of great excitement.

"Minister, have you heard the news?"

"How could I? I've only just got here. What is it?"

"We received a message from Admiral Story in Halifax and…"

"Yes?"

"There has been a huge explosion. A munitions ship caught fire and almost the whole city has been destroyed."

"What?"

"Yes, Minister. Apparently dozens of ships have been sunk and hundreds of businesses and houses have been demolished."

"How many dead?"

"Preliminary reports put it in the thousands."

"Great God! How did it happen?"

"The munitions ship—she was French, apparently —collided with a Norwegian vessel."

"Collided?"

"Yes, Minister."

"How the hell could ships collide in Halifax harbour?"

"It would seem to have been an error on the part of one or both of the pilots."

"I knew it!" Mewburn said violently. "Those redneck peasants couldn't pilot their way through a bathtub!"

"Well, Minister—"

"At last! This is just what we've been waiting for."

"Minister?"

"To take over the entire port! We discussed this some days ago, don't you remember?"

"Ah, yes."

"Right, Fiset. Call the Clerk of the Privy Council immediately and have him put the wheels in motion for an invocation of the War Measures Act for the purposes of bringing the entire port of Halifax under the control and command of the Government of Canada. And call the Prime Minister's office and arrange a call between him and me sometime today, if possible."

"Yes, at once, Minister."

"Now we can get rid of those local yokels and those meddling Brits."

"Minister, I wish you wouldn't use such intemperate language."

"I'm sure you do, Fiset. Typical civil servant. Softly softly is your style."

"Oh, sir—"

"Fiset, which of the two pilots was to blame?"

"It is not immediately apparent, Minister, but it would seem the pilot on the Norwegian vessel was in error."

"Have him arrested at once!"

"I can't do that, Minister. He's dead. He was killed along with the officers of the ship."

The Minister thought about this for a moment. "Alright. In that case, arrest the other one. Also set the wheels in motion for a judicial inquiry headed by a good judge, if you get my meaning."

"Oh, Minister, I think—"

"Fiset, don't mess me around on this. The Prime Minister will want this to be as clear-cut as possible. He won't want some wishy-washy, namby-pamby judge who sees all sides of the argument. This pilot —what was his name?"

"Mackey, I believe, sir."

"This Mackey was there when it happened. He and the French. The Norwegians are dead, so they can't stand trial. So the guilty parties must be the survivors."

"Minister, I would urge a certain degree of caution in this matter."

"Fiset, I will have someone's head for this, mark my word. You had better see it is not yours."

"Yes, Minister. I mean, no, Minister," Fiset said meekly.

Jeremy Akerman

21

Supporting a very shaky Douglas by the arm, Ronald Mackey limped and stumbled through pile after pile of building wreckage, moving beams and parts of walls whenever they could. They were not sure they were searching in the right place, not even that they were in the right street.

Whenever they saw a female body, they carefully checked the face, then moved on to the next. They knew it was their duty to find their Auntie Theresa, dead or alive.

~

With only shreds of his uniform still clinging to him, a battered and bleeding Admiral Chambers staggered down what was once a street. He thought it was the one on which his house was located, but all familiar landmarks had disappeared. On either side of him what was remaining of the buildings was in total shambles, none still with a roof and very few with any walls standing. From huge gashes in the road surface escaping gas gushed in fiery plumes.

On his uncertain way, the admiral encountered a number of human corpses, a dead horse still harnessed to a smashed wagon, an overturned street car, and several dogs, limping and whimpering.

Occasionally, Chambers passed survivors who were either calling for help or asking for the whereabouts of relatives. To those he was able to assist, he did what little he could, pulling them clear of rubble or tying a makeshift bandage. He had no comfort to offer those who were simply sitting in the dirt crying their hearts out.

To the others he could only shrug. He was in exactly the same situation as they were.

~

Ronnie and Dougie rounded the end of a huge tip of rubble and stopped, staring at a body partially covered with debris. This time, there was no doubt. Lying before them was their Aunt Theresa, her flaming red hair fanned out like a grotesque halo. They fell to their knees and wept inconsolably.

Tears ran down Ronnie's cheeks as he turned and looked up at the sky—where he had always been told God in his Heaven resided. The air was starting to clear of the previously pervasive black smoke. Snowflakes settled on his head and eyelashes. The tears started to turn to ice.

"Come on, Dougie. There's nothing we can do for them now. Let's go home and see if Ma is still alive."

He put his arm around Douglas and gently propelled the child out of the ruins and into the mangled street with its strange fires spurting from the potholes.

~

Gabriel and the stallion had reached the outer edges of the destruction area, where the buildings had sustained only broken windows, collapsed chimneys and missing roofs. The railway tracks they were following suddenly came to an end, rearing up, twisted and bent some ten feet in the air. Immediately beyond them was a yawning pit at least three yards long.

"There'll be no train coming through here any time soon," he said to the horse.

The snow lay heavily, slowing down the animal's progress into the city. An unnatural stillness prevailed, making the district seem devoid of all life but theirs. The corpses they encountered now were frozen solid. He nudged the horse along, more slowly because of the multitude of obstructions on the ground.

As he turned the corner into a street, he saw a makeshift crew of Canadian Reserve soldiers, searching the wreckage for survivors by shouting, "Anybody here?" They were calling out rather mechanically, Gabriel thought, as if it were a formality and they expected no response.

After watching this from a distance for a while, he started to trot on, but a sergeant jumped out from behind a pile of debris and pointed his rifle at Gabriel's chest.

"Halt! Who are you? What are you doing here? Get down from that horse. I bet it is stolen!"

"Listen, buddy," said Gabriel indignantly, "I am a lieutenant in the United States Navy. I'm stationed at Baker's Point. My plane fell into the drink up the Eastern Shore some days ago. I found this horse about ten miles back. It was running free."

"Where are you heading?"

"Back to base, eventually. But first I have to find my fiancée."

"Not so fast," said the sergeant. "It's just that we've been ordered to deal with looters."

"I'm not a looter. Look at me. I hardly have any decent clothes on. And I don't have any money. I spent my last nickel on a train ticket from Truro."

"The train! Did it stop before everything blew up here?"

"Yeah, with a few minutes to spare, I reckon."

"That's some good news, I guess."

"Not much of that going around."

"You got that right! Alright, I guess you can go. Good luck. I hope you find your fiancée."

"Thanks, sergeant. By the way, what do you do if you find any looters?'

"We shoot them."

"Shoot them? Dead?"

"Dead. Those are our orders."

~

Still half dazed, Admiral Chambers recognized some garden ornaments and a miraculously still-standing tree as belonging to his house, although the building itself was not identifiable. He picked his way through the wreckage and saw some of his books, torn to shreds and scorched, their multi-coloured covers strewn everywhere. He stood there in shock, wondering what had become of his family and staff.

Suddenly, he heard a voice shouting. "Get out of there, you fool!"

"What?" He turned and saw a city policeman.

"We have orders to shoot looters on sight."

"I am Rear Admiral Chambers of the Royal Navy. This is my house. Or rather, it used to be my house."

"Oh, I'm sorry sir, I didn't know. But now I look, I can see some kind of uniform."

"Yes, it's in a sorry state now, I'm afraid. Do you know what happened to my wife and servants?"

"I couldn't say, admiral. I know they took some people from here up to the dressing station."

"The dressing station? Where is that?"

"On the Commons, sir. I'd look for them there, if I were you."

"Thank you, constable. That's over a mile from here. With all the mess in the streets it'll take me hours to get there, so I'd best get started."

"Good luck, sir."

Chambers reached down and picked up a book which was less damaged than the others and tore out the inside page.

"Constable, do you have a pen I could borrow?"

"I've got this pencil, sir."

"Thank you. That is most kind. I want to leave a message for my niece so she will know where to find us—that is, if she is still alive."

He scribbled the note and casting about, saw there was a single post standing where the front gate had been. He could find no nails, so he tried to affix the note with one of his lapel insignia, but it didn't work.

"Why don't you try this, sir?" said the policeman, handing him a small rock.

Chambers thanked him, laid the note on top of the post, placed the rock on top, and then shuffled away.

~

Ronald and Douglas hobbled along a back street. All buildings in the vicinity had been obliterated, and the road was filled with holes and cracks.

They stopped in front of one gaping hole and peered down. About five feet below them they saw a man's body.

"He's dead for sure," said Dougie.

"Yeah. Dead as a doornail."

They moved off along the street. They did not know it, but they had just seen the corpse of Convoy Officer James Murray, who had given his life while gallantly trying to save others.

Also unknown to the boys, only streets away, their father was struggling through the smouldering desolation. Exhausted, hungry and dishevelled, he was dragging himself forward by sheer force of will, barely able to put one foot in front of the other.

~

As Gabriel rode into another street, he saw another squad of soldiers crowding around a Model T Tourer. The soldiers were rocking the car, while its driver cowered inside. The vehicle looked ridiculously out of place amid all the destruction and it was doubtful how far it could have gone in any direction. He cantered over to see what was going on.

"Listen here, kid," shouted one of the troops, "We're taking this car whether you like it or not. We need it to transport the wounded. Get out!"

"I have to go to my father's business and retrieve the cash box. He'll kill me if I don't." The driver was about eighteen and was shaking with fear.

"If you don't get out we'll kill you. We have the power to commandeer this vehicle!"

Uncertainly, the youngster climbed out. Unceremoniously, the soldiers piled into the car and drove away, driving crazily to avoid obstacles.

Gabriel dismounted and turned to the lad. "I could give you a ride. You'd have to jump up behind me. Where are you going?"

"To the sugar refinery" the boy said.

"I'm sorry to have to be the one to tell you this, but the refinery is gone. I passed by there earlier"

"Gone? What do you mean?"

"It was completely wiped out by the explosion. There's nothing left standing."

"Oh no! Dad will murder me." The boy sat down in the dirt, crying like a baby.

When Gabriel prepared to leave, the horse was gone. He looked around, and could just see him galloping away in the distance.

"Goodbye, my friend," Gabriel said softly.

~

Emma stood for a minute, staring at the blasted Naval Academy, marvelling at how its appearance had changed. The main gates were twisted and flung down, but still guarding the entrance intact were two stone lions looking sadly over the shattered city.

She pushed at a seemingly-solid door, but it collapsed immediately in a cloud of dust.

The Academy had fared better than most buildings in the vicinity, still possessing some of its walls and part of its roof. Inside it was dark and inexpressibly cold. Furniture, books, papers were strewn about the floor.

She wandered about the halls, and in and out of rooms, tripping over upturned chairs and desks. "William!" she shouted. "Are you here? Is anyone here?"

A young, handsome, blond naval instructor emerged from the shadows. He was badly cut and bruised. "Hello, miss. I'm the only one left. Everyone else has been taken up to the dressing station up at the Commons. They set up a relief centre there. I'm heading up that way myself. I came back for this." He held up a Scottish thistle pendant. "My mother gave it to me before she died."

"I am so sorry. There has been so much death."

"I don't mean now. She died in 1915."

"Oh, I see. Do you know William Chambers?"

"The admiral's nephew? Yes we all know Billy."

"Do you know…what happened to him…where he is?"

"I think he went with the others to the dressing station. Some of the youngsters were badly cut by flying glass. Some of them will never see again."

"Do you know if William, er, Billy was badly hurt?"

"I can't be sure, miss. Is Billy related to you?"

"Yes, he's my brother."

"Ah. I can see why you're so worried"

"I don't know what to do."

"Come with me to the Commons. If Billy's there, we'll find him. It looks like you could use some medical attention yourself."

"I'll be alright."

"My name's Gregory," he said, putting a protective arm around her and gently escorting her to the outside.

"I'm Emma."

"I'm pleased to meet you, Emma."

They slowly walked up the hill through the deepening snow. Emma could no longer feel her fingers, toes or nose and she prayed they would not be frostbitten. A horse-drawn cart passed by piled high with bodies. Emma shuddered.

"What about the Germans? Are they on their way here?"

"I don't know anything about Germans," said Gregory. "All this has been caused by a ship blowing up in the harbour."

"A ship? But—"

Her words were cut short by Gregory putting a hand on her arm. "Shhh. Listen. Do you hear something?"

A faint cry could be heard on the wind.

"It sounds like a child's voice."

"Come on, Emma. I think it is coming from over there. We'd better see if we can help."

Gregory led her off into the piles of rubble.

~

Mackey staggered on, tripping over the detritus which covered the streets. In the distance he saw a young man coming towards him.

"What a hell of a day!" said Gabriel. "Do you know what happened? Were we shelled by a German battleship?"

"No." Mackey shook his head sorrowfully. "I wish that's what did happen. There wouldn't have been this much destruction. There was a collision in the harbour and one of the ships—a munitions ship—went up."

"Good God! I've never seen anything like this. Have you lost anyone belonging to you?'

"I don't know yet. I'm heading home now to see if my family's alright. How about you?"

"Same thing. I am hoping to find my fiancée."

"Where have you come from?"

"From Harrigan's Cove," said Gabriel.

"Jesus. That's way up the eastern shore. You've come a long way."

"How about you?"

"I've only come from Dartmouth," said Mackey, although to him it had been like a thousand miles.

22

Ronnie and Dougie Mackey finally arrived at what used to be their home. The roof was gone and most of the walls had collapsed. The boys were bewildered and uncertain.

"Are you sure this is it?" Dougie asked.

"I dunno," replied his brother. "It's all different. I don't even know if this is the right street."

They grubbed around in the rubble for several minutes until Dougie shouted, "Ronnie! Look what I got. Ain't this one of yours?"

He held out a toy airplane, now much the worse for wear.

"That's mine, alright. This gotta be the place. We'd better check everything out more carefully."

They waded through masses of ceiling plaster as the dust blew up from underneath its coating of snow. As they approached the rear of the house, they heard faint cries.

"That sounds like Ma! Come on, Dougie, we got to dig her out."

~

Gabriel faced what he felt sure was the site of the Dominion Textile factory. He pushed through into what used to be the ground floor and looked about. With his boot, he idly pushed at a corpse which was lying in the filth. When it turned over, revealing a face mangled out of recognition, he gasped, fell to his knees and vomited.

Then he dragged himself to his feet and stumbled on.

Bodies were everywhere. Those which were female, he tenderly inspected, hoping against hope none of them would prove to be Emma.

He stopped, raised his head and shouted at the tops of his lungs. "Emma! Emma! Emma!"

No human sound responded, but he noticed that the wall between the two stairwells was starting to crumble and large pieces of masonry were falling with heavy plops into the snow.

Gabriel hastily withdrew from the building, falling over more bodies. He checked their faces and moved on. A little further on he tripped over a shattered beam and hurt his hand.

As he was pushing himself back up, he noted something shiny just beyond his hand. He immediately recognized the object as Emma's brooch. He picked it up, stuffed it into a pocket and set off with a renewed hope.

After about half an hour, he stood in front of the wreckage of the admiral's house. The place, such as it was, was bleak and deserted. He was about to move on when he noticed the rock on the gatepost. Something was protruding from under the rock and was flapping in the wind.

He removed the note which the admiral had left and brushed the snow off it. The paper was sodden so he could not read all of its contents, but he deciphered that it was addressed to Emma and made mention of the Commons.

As he was replacing the note, he heard a loud moan and, looking across the street, he saw a small boy tottering towards him. The boy reached out to Gabriel then collapsed at his feet.

He bent down and picked up the child in his arms. "You'd better come with me, little fellow. We'll see if we can get you fixed up somewhere."

Bearing his new-found burden, Gabriel moved slowly forward through the snow.

~

Emma and Gregory scrambled over the rubble in the direction of the crying. On the far side of the pile, they found a sort of tunnel in the ruins from which the sounds seem to be coming.

"I'm going in."

"No! It's too dangerous."

"I've no choice. I must go,"

"Well, please be careful!" Emma shivered. It seemed a long time since she had been able to feel her extremities.

"Here goes," said Gregory as he burrowed into the tunnel.

After some minutes, he reappeared. "It's a little girl. She's trapped under a joist. It's too heavy for me to shift by myself. We need to go and get help."

"But it's getting colder. If we leave her, she could freeze to death."

"Yes, of course, you're right. You'll have to come down with me and see if the two of us can move it."

"I suppose so."

"What's the matter?"

"I'm claustrophobic, but I'll give it a try."

"Good girl! Let's go."

They entered the tunnel and slowly edged along the narrow, confined space, following the child's cries. Halfway along the tunnel there was a creaking. They craned their necks listening and then the creaking turned into a loud crack as the tunnel collapsed, and they were pinned down by a large beam.

Then all was silent. The child's cries had stopped.

"Damn! Stupid thing!" Gregory cursed.

"It's no use. It's not going to budge."

Gregory stopped straining and lay back. Emma started to weep as the snow blew around them, collecting in their hair and clothing. Their faces were turning blue with the cold. They spoke with quiet, weakened voices.

"If I have to die, I'm glad it could be with you, Emma."

"That's sweet of you to say. I just wish I could see my fiancé one last time."

"Your fiancé? Is he a good man?"

"I think so. He was an American. We were going to be married when the weather gets warmer...but I suppose he's dead now."

"The must have been so many people killed by this explosion."

"He didn't die today. He was in an aeroplane crash. He was a pilot."

"I'm so sorry, Emma. I'm sorry he's dead."

"Soon we'll be dead, too."

~

The dressing station on the Commons was a large, hastily constructed marquee surrounded by a morass of mud and filthy slush. Soldiers were erecting new tents, and ambulances—some motorized but most horse-drawn—were bringing in more wounded by the minute.

Everywhere victims of the tragedy stood, sat, or lay, all displaying cuts or bruises or else freshly applied bandages. Some, in a state of shock, were staring vacantly into the distance. Some sat quietly whimpering to themselves. Some were in terrible pain and were groaning or screaming. Others, obviously blinded, sat, slowly shaking their heads.

Admiral Chambers staggered through the flap of the marquee and gaped at the vast array of misery in front of his eyes. He tried to accost several medical personnel, but they were too much occupied to be able to attend to him. This was not, he was acutely aware, a place where he could, or should, pull rank.

He wandered up and down the rows of injured, looking this way and that. When he reached the far end of the tent, he heard a voice calling him.

"Admiral! Admiral, over here!"

He whirled around to see a grotesque apparition limping towards him, supported on a crutch. It was Cameron, his butler. His head was swathed in bandages, his foot was in a cast and his arm was in a sling.

"Good God, man! Cameron, is that you? You look like absolute hell."

"So do you," said Cameron huskily. "You'll forgive me for saying so, sir, but I've seen you looking a whole lot better yourself!"

They laughed heartily, coughing and spluttering.

"I suppose you're right. But what of Mrs. Chambers and Marcus? Are they alright?"

"Master Marcus is fine. He is with Mrs. Hutchinson."

"And my wife?"

"She's right over here, sir, if you'll follow me."

Hobbling, he escorted the admiral to a corner of the marquee, where a nurse was applying iodine to Mrs. Chambers' wounds. She was in almost as bad shape as her husband and had a large, black patch over her right eye. Much to the nurse's annoyance, they attempted an awkward embrace.

"Mordie! Are you alright?"

"Just about in one piece, my dear. What news of Emma and William. Are they well?"

"William is over yonder, Mordie. He's been battered about a bit, but he'll survive. But I'm afraid there is no word on Emma. Do you think we should go looking for her?"

"Not a good idea, I think. We'd be a fine pair wandering around Halifax in a snowstorm. I left a note at the house...if she ever gets it...directing Emma to come here. All we can do is wait."

~

Gabriel surmounted a rise and saw the Commons ahead. Truth to tell, if he had not seen the big tents, troops and ambulances moving around, he would not have known where he was. So much of the city now seemed like undulating fields under a blanket of snow.

Large groups of people not deemed sufficiently injured to get medical attention were gathered around braziers for warmth, some of them trying to toast bread—and in a few cases, meat—at arm's length. Platoons of soldiers carried fresh loads of injured into the most recently erected tent. It looked more like the Battle of the Somme than Halifax.

He hitched the little boy up on his shoulder and went to the largest tent in search of a doctor.

"Excuse me," he said to a nurse who was scurrying by. She turned to him, seeing him holding out the child. "I found him in the street about half an hour ago."

"Is he conscious?"

"He was, but he collapsed in front of me. He hasn't regained consciousness since then."

"There's no regular doctor available right now," said the nurse hesitantly, "but you could give him to that man."

Gabriel looked to where the nurse indicated and saw a tall, black man, standing awkwardly on the sidelines.

"I don't understand."

"Don't tell anybody I told you, but he is a doctor from Jamaica. He has been treating people unofficially."

"Unofficially?"

"Yes, he has not been able to get medical privileges because—"

"Because he's black."

"Well…yes."

"Okay, I won't say anything. What's his name?"

"Ligoure. Dr. Ligoure."

"Thank you, nurse."

He waited until she had disappeared and then approached the black man.

"Dr. Ligoure?"

"Yes, that is I."

"I would be grateful if you could examine this child."

"Is he your son?"

"No, I found him in the street."

"Please bring him to the end of the tent. We should not attract too much attention."

"You are from Jamaica, Doctor? I've been there. I liked it very much."

"No."

"No?"

"No, I am from Trinidad. I don't think people around here have heard of it, that's why they all say I am Jamaican."

"Oh, I'm sorry."

"Don't be. Let us take a look at the patient."

Dr. Ligoure applied his stethoscope, then looked up sharply.

"My dear man," he said quietly, "this child has been dead for at least an hour."

Gabriel walked away, numb with grief. He stumbled along the rows, hardly knowing where he was. He aimlessly passed blood-soaked patients, some not even recognizable as human beings.

In a daze he wandered on until he bumped into a man. He looked and saw that it was Admiral Chambers. "Oh, hello, Admiral."

"Gabriel! Great Heavens. We thought you were finished when your plane went down. What are you doing here?"

"I brought somebody here. He's dead now."

"I am so sorry, my boy."

"But I was looking for Emma. Is she here?"

"Alas, no. William is alright, though." He nodded towards a bed where a badly injured boy was swaddled in bandages. "I left a note at the house, hoping she would find it and come here."

"I know. I found it. That's what led me here."

"There's been no sign of her yet. But don't lose heart, my boy. She'll probably come waltzing in here any minute."

"I must go."

"Don't be foolish. Look at you—you're all in. You must be exhausted."

"No, I have to find her."

"Where would you even look?" The Admiral remonstrated. "She could be anywhere. There's nothing you can do in this snow storm."

Gabriel shook his head, turned on heel and strode out of the tent. He went from one tent to another, asking everyone he saw if a young woman had been brought in. In the cases where the answer was in the affirmative, they took him to see the patients but none of them was his Emma.

He took aside one nurse and asked if she had been on duty all day and if so, had she seen his fiancée.

"No, she hasn't been brought in here, as far as I know. We don't know the names of half the people here…there's just too many. But I haven't seen anyone like the girl you described."

The nurse bustled away to turn back some stretcher bearers.

"No! There is no more room in here," she said

curtly, "You'll just have to take them somewhere else."

The grumbling stretcher bearers retreated back out into the cold. As they opened the flap, snow blew and scattered everywhere.

~

Emma and Gregory lay side by side, motionless. Their faces were increasingly blue, and snow stuck to their eyebrows and lashes.

~

Francis Mackey continued his tortuous journey through the devastated streets of Halifax's north end. He turned into his own street and started the long trudge home.

Ronnie and Dougie were straining at a large section of wooden and plaster walling which lay at a thirty degree angle on the rubble. Through a gash in the walling they could just see Lillian Mackey's cut and sweat-stained face beneath them.

"Don't worry, Ma. We'll get you out. Come on Dougie, give me a hand."

Grunting with the effort, they tried to dislodge the obstacle to their mother's release. The wall gave an inch or two, but then slid back into place.

Suddenly, Dougie looked around and saw his father coming up the street. "Daddy! Daddy!"

"Hello there Dougie. Hello Ronnie. What are you doing?"

"Trying to get Ma out of here!"

Frank hugged the lads, then poked his head into the hole. "Just look at yourself, Lillian," he said. "I can't leave you for five minutes without you getting into all kinds of trouble."

Jeremy Akerman

23

"Frank Mackey, you get me out of here this very minute!" said a frustrated Lillian from under the rubble.

"Hold on there, girl. Come on, boys, give your old man a hand."

The three of them bent down and grabbed the chunk of walling and heaved. After a few minutes there was a ripping sound, and it broke off, sending the boys reeling.

Mackey reached down and carefully pulled Lillian up through the opening. They embraced tearfully and their sons joined them in a family hug.

"Now then, mother," said Mackey. "Where are the others?"

"I'm not sure, Frank. I passed out just after it happened. They were somewhere around the house at the time."

"Poor little girls. I pray to God we ain't lost them."

"Oh, don't say that, Frank. Let's go look for them."

"It won't be easy in all this snow, but we won't

rest until we know what happened to them. Come on, lads."

The four of them explored the site as best they could, pulling, pushing, lifting and kicking at pieces of their former house.

Finally, when they were about to give up in despair, Ronnie came up to his father. "Dad?"

"Yes, son?"

"If the girls is dead would their ghosts haunt us?"

"What are you talking about? What nonsense is this?"

"Over there in back. I heard something right spooky. I thought it might be a ghost."

"Where? Show me!"

They struggled through the debris towards what had been the yard. In front of them they could see the bottom of a wardrobe covered by a large piece of heavy panelling.

"Is this it?"

"Yeah. Listen!"

They bent down and, sure enough, a moaning sound came up to them. This was quickly followed by a knocking.

Mackey burst out laughing. "Ghosts my Aunt Fanny! Come on, Ronnie, let's get them out of there!"

They shifted the panel to reveal a relatively-un-scathed wardrobe underneath. The door was stuck, but Mackey managed to pry it open with his knife.

There staring up at them, like sardines in a can, were Mary, Marjorie and Lilly, quivering with cold and fear, but all intact. One by one, the girls clambered out and, after giving their father a quick hug, ran to their mother.

"Everyone present and accounted for!" Mackey said. "Thank the Lord for sparing us. Now, Lillian, we've got to find shelter."

"If we head toward St. Agnes parish we might find something along the way," Lillian said, "Maybe there's still buildings in one piece."

~

The storm was intensifying as Gabriel desperately flailed his way through drifts and wreckage. Periodically he paused, peering into ruined buildings, shouting into the white wind, "Emma! Emma! Emma!"

He rounded a corner and encountered a troop of soldiers surrounding an apparent looter, who was tied to a post.

"Didn't you know the order has been given to shoot looters on sight?" demanded a corporal.

"No...no... it was only a box of cigars," The looter pleaded. "They were just sitting there. I'll give them back. I'll do anything. Please don't shoot me."

"That's too bad for you, chum. Your looting days are over."

The corporal raised his rifle to the looter's head and pulled the trigger. The man slumped in a disgusting splatter of blood and brains.

The corporal wiped off his uniform with a handkerchief. "Let's go, boys!"

As they moved off, some of the soldiers were laughing. Revolted, Gabriel started to sob as he shuffled off into the thickening storm.

Shortly, he passed a group of men and women who were searching through ruins, combing the debris for signs of their loved ones. Almost as if in a daydream, he moved on without acknowledging their presence. A little further on, he heard a shout from a man who was digging in a pile of snow.

"Help! Come quick! I've got two in here!"

Another man pushed past Gabriel and rushed towards the first man. Gabriel paused, then followed him.

"Are they alive?" asked the second man.

"It's kind of hard to say. It sure doesn't look like it."

Some more rescuers arrived and joined in the effort. He watched as they struggled, shifting pieces of masonry, plaster and wood. They took hold of a huge beam and heaved it to one side.

"Alright," said the first man, "We're clear. Let's get them out."

The rescuers carefully extracted the first body, a young man and laid him to one side.

"This one's dead."

"How about the other one?"

"There's a chance, I reckon. There are still signs of life. Not much, but some."

They took out the second person, a woman, and carried her over the snow, knocking her hat off as they went. Staring at them through the snow, Gabriel saw a mass of golden hair fall and sweep along the ground.

"Emma! My Emma!"

He raced forward and tried to seize her from the rescuers. The men roughly pushed him away.

"What the hell do you think you're doing? Get the fuck away from here!"

"That's Emma. She's my fiancée."

"Oh. Okay, fella. Here she is. Be careful. It looks as if she is in bad shape."

Gabriel took her from the man and, holding her in his arms, he wept. "Emma. Oh, Emma."

Emma did not respond. Tears streamed down his face, freezing in the stubble of his beard. "Oh, Emma, I love you so much…the whole world has gone mad…

everything is destroyed…I saw them shoot a man…it was terrible…oh, Emma, please don't die."

Gradually, weakly, Emma's eyes opened. Her voice was very tiny and strained. "Gabriel?"

Incredulous, he sobbed with joy and hugged her tightly. Then picking her up, he turned and headed back to the Commons. "My darling girl. I am going to take you where you can have help and get well again."

The rescuers applauded as Gabriel staggered away.

24

Almost a quarter of the cities of Halifax and Dartmouth were completely levelled. Several square miles of smoking rubble now occupied what were previously thriving residential, industrial and mercantile communities. The harbour and its approaches, together with Bedford Basin, were cluttered with sunk, wrecked and otherwise damaged vessels.

Before he was recalled by the British Admiralty and transferred to Quebec City, Admiral Bertram Chambers was given a preliminary report as to the damage caused by the explosion. The estimates were that some 25,000 people were left without proper shelter and over 6,000 were completely homeless. About 1,600 buildings had been totally destroyed and another 12,000 were damaged. Over 2,000 people had been killed, a further 9,000 were injured and about 200 were blinded, most by flying glass.

In 1918, the Government of Canada invoked the War Measures Act and took complete control of the port and harbour. It was an unnecessary move since, officially, they had received control as far back as 1903. Such was the pettiness and jealousy that, even in the days immediately following the explosion, they were still arguing about what Admiral Chambers, an Englishman, should be called, and proposed the alternative title of Port Convoy Officer and Senior Officer of Escorts Halifax to describe his responsibilities. They were said to include control of any Imperial vessels visiting port in connection with escort work. This made it clear that he would have no jurisdiction over Canadians.

The admiral's son, Marcus Chambers, later became a famous racing car driver in Britain.

An extensive investigation and a series of inquiries were held into the causes of the disaster. In an act of supreme irony and spite, Francis Mackey was arrested, along with Captain Le Medec of *Mont Blanc*, and they were charged with manslaughter and criminal negligence in the death of *Imo*'s pilot, William Hayes. But later, Supreme Court Justice Benjamin Russell determined the charges were unfounded and ordered Mackey released.

However, the Government of Canada, once it had its man, did not intend he should go completely unpunished, so they refused to restore Mackey's license. This meant that he never worked again as a pilot.

Neither the government nor the people of Halifax, who had been whipped into a frenzy by politicians and the media, had any intention of being fair or even neutral. Someone had to suffer for the devastation and they were not particular as to who that would be. Mackey was the only survivor of the two ships involved in the collision who was still in Canada, so where else could they turn to find a scapegoat? His name was smeared and he was scorned even by those he had known for years.

~

Gabriel and Emma were married the following year and moved to Virginia. There, Gabriel was promoted to Commander and later to Captain. He and Emma had three children. The eldest, a girl, was named Theresa.

Jeremy Akerman

25

Since no minutes were kept, the exact date cannot be stated, but some time before Christmas in 1917, an extraordinary meeting took place in the office of Kaiser Wilhelm II in his capacity of Commander-in-Chief of the Imperial Germany Army and Navy.

It was a vast, heavily-gilded, sumptuously-furnished room on which an exaggerated military presence and character had been imposed. In addition to large portraits of Frederick the Great of Prussia, Frederick Barbarossa and Otto von Bismarck, the walls were covered in maps and charts. The gold, carved tables were strewn with battle positions, aerial photographs and various official orders. In small oases among the documents were plates filled with the Kaiser's favourite red sausage and spicy Liptauer cheese spread paired with bread.

The Kaiser sat behind a huge desk, bristling with a mixture of importance and impatience. He was small man in his fifties, visually unremarkable except for a withered arm and spiked moustaches. He kept bobbing up and down as she spoke, and often gave the impression that he was about to come over the desk in his anger.

Seated wearily before him was the nominal army Chief of Staff, Paul von Hindenburg, a heavy, tired man of 70, wearing a thick moustaches which joined heavy mutton chops on his cheeks. Hindenburg had long since ceased to be the real power behind the throne, and was sick of war and of life.

The real power in Germany was now being wielded by army Quartermaster General Erich von Ludendorff, who stood some feet away, looking out of the Chancellery window. Ludendorff was a tall, imposing, canny man is his mid-sixties.

Excitedly, the Kaiser rattled out his orders like a machine gun while Hindenburg did his best to write them down. At length, the Kaiser picked up a piece of paper and studied it carefully. "*Mein Gott in Himmel*! Have you seen this, Hindenburg? An enormous explosion has occurred at one of the Allies' most important convoy ports. It says tremendous damage. Vast loss of life. Will take months for the port to be operational again. It is about time we had some good news!"

Wearily, Hindenburg took the paper and read it. "That is excellent, Your Majesty. It will be a serious blow to their supply lines."

"Indeed! It could hardly have been better if we had done it ourselves."

He paused and glanced over at Ludendorff, who was still staring out of the window.

The Kaiser frowned. "We didn't have anything to do with it, did we, Ludendorff?"

Ludendorff turned slowly and gave the Kaiser an ambiguous look as he ever so slightly shrugged his shoulders.

THE END

Afterword

Readers will quickly come to the conclusion that I regard the main character, Francis Mackey, as a hero—which was certainly not how he was seen at the time. If I have gone overboard in portraying him in a positive light, it is because I think we owe him something in death that he did not get in life. There is no doubt in my mind that Mackey was set up, framed, took the rap for the crimes of others, and suffered the consequences for many years.

For the record, the following characters are purely my own invention: Emma and William Chambers, Gabriel Hanson, Nigel Gilchrist, Harold, Doris Hector and Margaret Wambolt, Jerimiah Borden, Mrs. Hutchinson, Theresa Wrayton, Moreau, Pitcairn, Carter, Wilcox, Benson, MacQueen, Cooper, Cameron, Gregory, and Wright.

Those who want pure history should consult the excellent *Shattered City: The Halifax Explosion and the Road to Recovery* by Janet Kitz, and *Aftershock: The Halifax Explosion and the Persecution of Pilot Francis Mackey* by Janet Maybe.

Jeremy Akerman

About the author

Jeremy Akerman is an adoptive Nova Scotian who has lived in the province since 1964. In that time he has been an archaeologist, a radio announcer, a politician, a senior civil servant, a newspaper editor and a film actor.

He is painter of landscapes and portraits, a singer of Irish folk songs, a lover of wine, and a devotee of history, especially of the British Labour Party.